THE REBEL AND
THE HEIRESS

When Tom Tolley, ex-Confederate fighter in the Civil War returns home to the family farm in Arizona, he is met with flying lead . . . The heiress is Mary-Ann, daughter of millionaire Huey J. Charters. Sparks fly when Tom, dispossessed of his farm, meets the impish heiress. But they are thrown together against a hostile town, a scheming murderer and the secretive Jed Carbone. Can Mary-Ann's wilful nature be turned into courage when events take a gruesome turn?

CHAP O'KEEFE

THE REBEL AND THE HEIRESS

Complete and Unabridged

LINFORD
Leicester

First published in Great Britain in 2005 by
Robert Hale Limited
London

First Linford Edition
published 2006
by arrangement with
Robert Hale Limited
London

British Library CIP Data

O'Keefe, Chap
    The rebel and the heiress.—Large print ed.—
Linford western library
    1. Western stories
    2. Large type books
    I. Title
    823.9′14 [F]

    ISBN 1–84617–206–3

Published by
F. A. Thorpe (Publishing)
Anstey, Leicestershire

Set by Words & Graphics Ltd.
Anstey, Leicestershire
Printed and bound in Great Britain by
T. J. International Ltd., Padstow, Cornwall

This book is printed on acid-free paper

1

Shooting Sheriff

Tom Tolley kneed the sweat-lathered black gelding on to the long downward path into the valley. Both man and beast were grateful for the shafts of shade cast by the ever-thicker stands of pine that dotted the red rock slopes. A hot Arizona sun had blazed down on them many hours from a sky of glaring blue, making the uphill ride a chore that Tom was glad would soon be over.

His shoulders were slumped, and the horse's gait was plodding, every lift of its hoofs a visible effort. Long miles behind them were reason enough for their weariness.

Home at last! Tom remembered every last detail of the thousand acres of marginal farmland, half in timber, on which he'd spent most of his boyhood.

But it was four long years since he'd last ridden this trail. Much had happened in them, including a bloody civil war. Home would be changed, like most everything. His widower father had died two years back in '63. The homestead would be abandoned, the cultivated land weed-choked, no question.

Would he be able yet to sit on the porch and imagine he could still hear the lilting song and smell the fresh floral perfume of his ma, as he had during his melancholy teenage years when she was dead of consumption and gone, hopefully to eternal rest?

Tom imagined house and barn would need repairs before he'd be free again to lie back and indulge in bitter-sweet porch memories.

The trail forked and Tom took the lesser path to the left, away from the just-visible creek that threaded the valley bottom. The watercourse gave its name to Soldier Creek, the township situated down the road apiece to the right. Beyond, a range of jagged mountains encircled the high valley on three sides. Behind, in the lower altitudes to the south, cacti- and scrub-grown badlands sprawled to the Mexican border and on.

'Come on, old hoss,' Tom urged. He leaned over and patted his animal's neck. 'Soon enough there'll be rest and water aplenty for the two of us.'

He'd taken off his stained old hat and was flapping it by its twisted brim to cool his burning face. So when the Tolley place came into sight around one of the towering boulders scattered haphazardly on the valley slopes dwarfing even the pines that grew amongst them, the surprise was akin to and abrupt as a rabbit pulled from a conjurer's hat.

In a wave of his damp headgear, it was all before him. Tom saw not the welcoming shapes of house and barn silhouetted against blue sky and flanking trees. He saw a heap of charred beams, broken roof shingles and smashed cladding. Only the fire-blackened stack of the stone chimney still stood among the debris, pointing upwards like a sick monument to his past life and dreams.

'Goddamn! The old place has been torched,' he muttered.

Tom knew that during the War Between the States two companies of blue-clad California Volunteers, Unionists, had been posted hereabouts, though somewhat to the north. In the year his pa had died, Congress and President Lincoln, fearful of a Confederate takeover, had made Arizona a territory of the Union. A governor and his entourage of Washington-appointed subordinates had arrived in the country from back East.

But this destruction of the humble property of an absentee owner didn't smack of official action.

'More likely some local vigilante hotheads fancying the bluebellies' cause, I reckon,' Tom told himself.

At the time he'd left Soldier Creek to

join the Confederate army, the Texan lieutenant-colonel John R. Baylor had defeated the Union soldiers at Fort Fillmore and declared a Confederate Territory of Arizona with himself its self-proclaimed military governor.

But sympathies among the Arizonans had been split. After several encounters with Union forces, the Confederates had been forced to withdraw to Rio Grande in south-west Texas. The allegiance to the Confederacy sworn by the citizens of Tucson and Mesilla in March 1861 had been brought to nothing in little over a year.

Those Arizonans like Tom, who stuck to wearing a grey uniform, retreated someplace else to do their fighting.

Tom drew rein on the black, leaned back in the saddle, put one hand on the cantle, and turned to look around him — back down the dusty trail shimmering in the heat haze, into the shade of the trees, up to the rim of the rock slopes. Of course, his inspection revealed no lurking arsonists. But at that moment it seemed to him it saved his life.

For, as he turned, he felt the hot wind of a heavy slug whip past his bare head. It was followed on the instant by the vicious crack of a rifle, then the snarling whine of a ricochet off a trailside sandstone boulder — and an ugly symphony of shattering echoes of both sounds that rang through the valley.

Whether it was the gunflash, the zipping lead, the sudden cacophony, or the tug of the bit as Tom involuntarily jerked on the reins, the tired black reared steeply, whinnying alarm.

The horse pranced on its hind legs and Tom found his saddle tipped from horizontal to vertical. He dropped the reins, grabbed for the horn, missed it. His feet left the stirrups and he was airborne.

It had all happened so quickly, too quickly. The ground rushed up to meet him and he struck it with sickening, bone-jarring force.

His senses fragmented in a starburst of lights that was absorbed by the pitch black of unconsciousness.

* * *

He came round again slowly. He'd no way of knowing how long he'd lain senseless, but he didn't think too much time could have passed. The impact still throbbed through his dumped body. He felt weak. Pale, nauseous. But his assailant had made no attempt to finish him off with a second shot.

He lay still; waited with the phlegmatic calm of a man who has known and survived enemy fire when others around him, more foolhardy, have leaped up and died.

Approaching boots crunched on the crushed rock that paved what had been the front yard of the Tolley farm.

'All right, feller,' a voice said. 'I didn't aim to kill you. Just to give you a scare is all. You can stop playing possum and get to your feet.'

Cautiously, Tom lifted his head and body, taking the weight on his elbows and spread hands.

The man who'd bushwhacked him was a loose-jointed, round-shouldered gent of about forty in knee-length spurred boots. He had a hawkish face and a close-trimmed smear of moustache. A metal star glinted on his vest. In his hands was a rifle: a big beast, forty-seven inches in all, a Spencer lever-action repeater made to hold seven .50-calibre rimfire cartridges in a tube magazine in the buttstock.

His looks were vaguely known to Tom. Searle . . . George Searle that was his name, though he hadn't worn the sheriff's badge when Tom had left the Soldier Creek country.

Tom got himself up, letting his hand hover over the butt of the .44 Colt Army revolver on his thigh.

'Don't touch that six-shooter, or I will blast you, boy,' the star-packer said.

'For why?' Tom demanded. 'And what's your reason for shooting from

8

ambush the first time?'

'You're a trespasser, that's why. There's already been a varmint of that stripe skulking about this property, and I'm minded to see no more, y'understand?'

'I ain't a trespasser. This is the Tolley homestead, or what's been left of it, and I'm Tom Tolley, back from the war.'

Searle narrowed his eyes, but the hard look didn't leave them. 'Well now, is that so? Thought you looked kind of familiar. I got a good eye for faces. A Reb, huh?'

'An ex-Reb, Mister Sheriff. The war's over.'

Searle spat on the ground. 'Dirty Secesh trash, put it anyways you choose. They should've hanged all those sons. Hell, greyback, you better ride back where you came from. You ain't welcome in Soldier Creek, for sure.'

'Then I'll stick here, on the Tolley property.'

'No you won't, boy, on account of this place no longer is your'n.'

Tom stiffened. 'Of course it's mine. I inherited on my pa's death.'

'That's a coupla years back,' Searle said, shaking his head, grinning a bit beneath his little moustache. 'Before your pappy died he paid his land taxes in Confederate coin. Such payments were declared invalid and a Yankee judge put the place up for auction to clear the debt. You own damn all, boy.'

'That can't be right, not in Arizona!' Tom protested. He swore furiously for several seconds, cursing nameless two-timing, double-crossing, turn-coat citizenry.

The sheriff guffawed. 'There's no future for a Reb in these parts,' he drawled. 'Your little parcel of land was bought at auction by Mayor Saul Pelzer, no less. You lost it, farm boy.'

Tom picked up his curly brimmed hat and whacked it against his leg, raising dust. 'We'll see about that. I reckon you're running a bluff. Any title your mayor holds can't be worth the paper it's writ on.'

He knew next to nothing about land

deeds or courts, but he had every confidence in his moral right to what had been the Tolley farm.

'Fighting talk, huh?' Searle said. He turned to Tom's horse, standing patiently on dropped reins. 'This crow-bait belong to you?'

'Sure it does. I'm not a horse-thief. And it's not crow-bait. It's fine cayuse. Considerable fine.'

'Yeah?' Searle jeered. 'That must be why it dumped you.'

'You were the cause of that, thick-head.'

'More tough-guy talk! Point of fact, I figure I oughta take this off you, too.' Searle hoisted the Henry rifle from the boot slung alongside Tom's saddle and dropped it on the ground. 'I wouldn't want you to get your fiery self into no gunplay.' Then he swung the muzzle of his Spencer, pointing it at Tom's middle. 'And I'd be obliged if you'd hand over that there belt-gun, the Colt.'

'Why the devil should I?' Tom said, feeling his gorge rise.

11

'One, because a .50 slug in the gut is mighty painful. Two, because Rebs can't bear arms, like they can't vote. It's a condition of their parole.'

'Bullshit! You've got your facts wrong, Searle. That don't apply here.'

But Tom unbuckled the gunbelt and let his handgun fall, not wanting to risk injury or death with none to witness the injustice of his fate.

'Ain't nothing wrong with my facts in this bailiwick, Tolley. Mayor Pelzer told me — Rebs have signed an Ironclad Oath of allegiance to the Union in exchange for their freedom. Greybacks get no vote; they carry no guns.'

Searle picked up the firearms and whistled. A bay mare emerged from back in the wood where it had been hidden up. Searle stashed the guns, put a foot in a stirrup and swung up into the saddle.

'Goodbye, Reb,' he said. 'Don't let me find you here when I ride by again. In fact, it'd be real smart to pull your freight right outa the territory like your ass was afire.'

'By God,' Tom growled to his departing back, 'I ain't hightailing it anywhere on your say-so.'

* ★ ★

Tom led his horse over to the shade of the timber, sat on a rock and inhaled deep, calming breaths of the scent of the sun-heated pine.

He hadn't much liked any part of what he'd heard from the sheriff. After General Lee had surrendered to General Grant at Appomattox, Virginia, Tom had expected the whole nation to put behind it gladly the years of hatred and killing. He'd looked forward himself to resettling peaceably and working the Tolley farm. But though he distrusted Searle, it sounded like that was not to be. The courts were dominated by opportunists. In some places Yankee carpetbaggers were moving in.

Was the Saul Pelzer who'd grabbed

his land one of them?

Possibly not.

Racking his brain, trying to remember, Tom seemed to recollect a local businessman of a similar if not the same name. He'd not been mayor, though, any more than Searle had been sheriff. The Pelzer he recalled had owned the livery stable in Soldier Creek.

'What the hell . . . ?'

Tom's restless eye detected sudden movement among the heap of ash and charcoal that had once been his home. Like some burrowing animal was surfacing amidst it.

A whole square-shaped section of the black debris was lifting. But Tom knew better than to suppose for more than a first moment that the phenomenon was caused by subterranean wildlife.

The rising structure of warped and scorched boards was the remains of a trap-door that had in former times given entry to a root cellar dug out under the house. When he was a boy, the cellar had been a cool storage place for fruit, vegetables and bottles of preserves. It was also one of his favourite hideyholes.

But who was using it now?

2

An Unlikely Helper

A clutching hand appeared in the widening gap between the rising two-inch lumber and the ground around it. Then a head — crowned with a hat, more battered and dirty than Tom's, over matted strands of greying, collar-length hair.

The heavy trap-door fell back raising a cloud of soot, and the apparition clambered out. The rest of his rig was as disreputable as his hat. A ragged-hemmed, claw-hammer coat covered what might once have been a fancy vest. A grubby flannel shirt was complemented incongruously by a straggly string tie.

Tom went over. Closer up, the man was even less pretty. In truth, he was a pitiful wreck. He was stoop-shouldered, his beard was tangled and nicotine-yellowed, his eyes red, his nose puffy and veined. Worse, he smelled as only an unwashed, habitual drinker smells.

'Who might you be, mister?' Tom asked. He was tired and still angered by his clash with Sheriff Searle. His tone was sharp. 'An' by what rights are you here?'

The old man hawked and wiped his whiskers with the back of his unclean hand. 'Carbone's the handle,' he rasped. 'Jed Carbone.' He uttered a short whinny which Tom took for a laugh. 'Rights? Squatter's rights is all I got.'

'You'd better not let Sheriff Searle find you here.'

'Yeah, son, I hear'd an' saw some o' thet. I lifted the trap a smidgeon an' peeked out. 'Tain't no wonder yuh're bitter.'

'This place was my home before the war. It's wonderful in the valley. When the sun's on the mountain peaks round about, it has a kind of solemn grandeur.

A peace.' Hearing himself, Tom felt slightly embarrassed by his eloquence. 'Sure, the country is rugged in parts and calls for a hardy spirit when times are bad. But I liked it here and had pleasant memories.'

'Yuh're right, son. Things here in God's open could suit a man jest dandy. But I bin spendin' time in thet town up the crick when they don't run me out unjus'ly. Thar's goin's-on thar thet jest ain't proper.'

Tom realized the old man, drunk and vagrant though he might he, could be an unbiased source of up-to-date information. 'Tell me, what do you know about Saul Pelzer?'

Jed Carbone scratched himself, making Tom think of fleas and kindred nasties. 'Like Searle says, he's mayor. But he's a heap more t' boot. It ain't jest the livery he owns. He's tooken over the town's biggest mercantile an' its hotel. Reckon he's out t' git a hold over most every other property, too.'

'How will he manage that? I mean, I

appreciate he's twisted the law to grab this farm, but that won't wash with the townies' businesses, surely?'

Old Jed whinnied another laugh. 'Yuh gotta believe it, son. I hear he gives them thar tricky mortage loans. Seems the conditions is so drafted by his shyster lawyers that them who borrers is certain-sure t' default. He has 'em under his boot-heel by means of whosoevers and whereases.'

'Hell, that's too bad. I was hoping I might rustle up some support for reclaiming my land.'

'Naw, they'll be swayed by Pelzer, seein's they ain't in no position t' dare buck him. O' course, they won't admit thet. They'd be like Searle — say it's on account o' your bein' a Reb. All un-re-con-structed an' sich.' Jed stumbled over the long word.

'There must be some law I can call on . . . ' Tom said. Thought creased his darkened brow.

'Waal, I guess it don't settle none too easy with me neither, but yuh seen

Searle an' he stands in too well with Pelzer, the mayor bein' chairman of the peace committee thet does the appointin' o' the sheriff.'

'Yeah, Searle sounded like he was in Pelzer's pocket right enough. But what does a guy who aims to be the bigshot politician want with a farm like mine? Ma and pa scraped a living off it, but we were always dirt-poor.'

'I can't say, son, not yet. But I ain't no duffer. Mebbe I kin l'arn it in town. You go inta Soldier Crick an' they'll run yuh out on Searle's say-so. Me now, I'm jest a town drunk they's seen afore.'

'You mean you'll go in there and put your ear to the ground for me?' Tom asked.

' 'Xactly, son. I likes the cut o' your jib. Yuh loan me a mite o' coin t' cover victuals an' a feed-sack o' cracked oats fer my burro, an' I'll go t' town an' nose around, listen good.' He added magnanimously, 'Meantime, yuh kin hide out in the root cellar.'

Tom wondered whether the old man

might not be leading him a dance. The burro, for instance. He looked around, checking. 'I see no burro, Mr Carbone.'

'Heh-heh! Nor did thet fool sheriff!' Jed hopped gleefully from one split-booted foot to the other. 'Foller me, son.'

He headed off back of the site of the destroyed homestead and into the nearest wood. A narrow bridle path wound through a tangle of undergrowth to a hide, constructed with the skill of a woodsman so that it could be picked out only by the sharpest searching eye.

When it heard the men coming up, a burro poked its head out from a cleverly woven screen of dead and living evergreen boughs and sticks, long ears cocked. It had the typical, big-eyed, woebegone expression of its species.

Tom said, 'I'm amazed the beast didn't sound off when Searle and me came poking around. There was the gunshot, too.'

'A knowin' critter is Martha. She don't scare easy. Fact is, she don't do much o' anythin' less'n she's of a mind to. Like some wimmin, this burro. Needs persuadin' somethin' awful.'

Tom shook his head wonderingly from side to side. 'You know, it'd mean a whole lot to me if you really could find out what's afoot here. I need a great deal more information; the chance to rest up, too.'

He pushed aside the last of his misgivings and reached a bold decision. 'Come back to my horse. I do have some dollars left in my warbag. You're welcome to what you'll need in town if it'll put me on the trail to getting this business sorted.'

The money handed over, the old man brought a pack up from the cellar and threw it on to Martha. The burro peeled back her thick lips and showed her teeth, but was co-operative enough when Jed rode out. 'I'll be back afore it's full dark tomorrow,' he said.

Tom watched them go, the burro stomping off with tucked-in tail and flattened ears.

But when he went down into the forgotten cellar to look around, he was assailed by new doubts. Had he made a mistake in giving Jed Carbone money? America was officially off the gold standard and he'd given Jed some of the precious paper dollars, greenbacks that had been issued by President Lincoln's government during the war. Had he been taken for a sucker?

Though the cellar showed evidence of the squatter's use, something was missing. It bothered Tom that he couldn't put his finger on what.

★　★　★

The girl in the dining-room of the St James Hotel picked idly at her steak, the house specialty, and took only infrequent helpings from the accompanying cut-glass bowls of vegetables, potatoes and salad. Nor did she pay much attention to the conversation of her two male companions, the elder of whom shared her sandy colouring and was plainly her father.

Most of the time she spent staring out the window at the Soldier Creek main-street scene, though she did sometimes take a sip from a tall glass of iced tea, and she did occasionally twist an idle finger in a lock of her hair. Its shiny mass of thick, red-gold curls cascaded to her shoulders but was cut straight across her unlined young forehead. A freckle or three added interest where the creamy skin of her forehead met the bridge of a charmingly tip-tilted nose.

'What have you got your pretty blue eyes on out there, Mary-Ann dear?' asked the man who wasn't her father. He was a big, thickset man with a tight-lipped mouth and square-jawed, resolute face. The solicitous enquiry sounded out of place on a tongue that might have been made for the issuing of harsh orders, and his dark gaze stayed cold and assessing even as it drank in the girl's beauty.

Mary-Ann sighed. 'Nothing, I guess, Mr Gipson.'

'Aw, really, dear . . . you must drop the mister and learn to call me Virgil, I know your pa would like that. And after the three of us have travelled so far together to be here, it seems kind of foolish to be standing on ceremony.'

Mary-Ann was reminded of the long, butt-jarring miles to this isolated hick township, spent sitting on the ineffectually padded seats of a Concord coach with leather thoroughbraces for its suspension.

It had been an unusual experience for the pampered daughter of a self-made millionaire who doted on her, but she'd humoured her daddy's whimsical yet touching determination that she should come along and so be kept in his sight and get to know better his right-hand mines manager, Virgil Gipson.

'Very well, Virgil Gipson then,' she said, and turned back to the passing parade of Soldier Creek.

Gipson scowled. 'Just Virgil will do. And what is it out there that's so damned interesting?'

'Nothing important,' she said, wincing slightly at the 'damned' which she thought unnecessary in a lady's company; indicative of low breeding. 'Just a bleary-eyed old hobo, the worse for drink I would guess.'

Again she looked out pityingly at the shambling derelict in the dusty claw-hammer coat. He was weaving his way across the main street toward the hotel's doors, a drunken flush on his unhealthy face.

He swayed from her sight and she heard the clump of his boots as he came up on to the boardwalk. 'The poor fellow,' she said.

Gipson grunted. 'Your concern scarcely does you credit, Mary-Ann. By the man's garb and appearance, I'd say he was a one-time prospector. I've only scorn for that entire class — never seen one that was worth a damn. Fools like that spend a lifetime scratching in the dirt and wind up with nothing, endlessly trying to cadge a grubstake or, in this case, drink, I reckon. If one of my mine workers got in such a state I'd see to it he was thrashed and discharged.'

'I'm sure you'd take pleasure in doing it personally,' said Mary-Ann with sweet sarcasm.

The mine manager laughed. 'You're nothing if not sassy, my dear.'

'Now, you two,' her father said. 'Stop teasing one another. You know, Mary-Ann, Virgil is my most trusted lieutenant. One day he'll probably run the Charters empire for me. And you, Virgil, I'll expect you to maintain my daughter's comfortable life for her after I'm gone, as I'm sure you will.'

Mary-Ann cringed inwardly. Did Daddy have to make his fence-mending and ridiculous matchmaking so obvious? Gipson was a cold fish at best; a vicious bully at worst. Sure, Gipson might be the ideal right-hand man in her father's ruthless world of big business, but it irritated her that he, Huey J. Charters, the man who'd built a fortune out of nothing, could be so blind to her feelings in the matter of Gipson's personal unattractiveness.

The sounds of altercation in the adjoining lobby broke into her thoughts.

'I'm powerful hungry, Mr Bloody Lobby Clerk,' said a voice picking its words with exaggerated care. 'I need vittles!'

'Sir, you're not fit to enter the hotel's dining-room. You're some liquored up. The gentlefolk — '

'Git your han's offa me! Yuh dassent push Jed Carbone were he a younger feller, tha's a fac'. Yuh ain't got no respect!'

In the dining-room, Gipson curled his lip in contempt. 'Throw the dirty bum out,' he growled, as unheard encouragement to the hotel worker.

Mary-Ann knew he was also winding her up, to see if he could provoke an inflammatory reaction from her that might upset her father and push him into taking a stronger line over her perceived wilfulness. He was a devious swine, was Gipson!

She decided she'd show him.

Throwing down her table napkin, she flounced from the table, head held high, curls bouncing, and went out into the lobby.

The drunk was counting out dollar bills on to the high counter from a roll held in a grubby fist. 'See,' he said with triumphant owlishness, 'I got *dinero* in my poke — lotsh and lotsh o' greenbacks.'

The clerk raised his hands in refusal, backing away. 'Sir, I must insist you leave. We can't take your money — '

'Oh, for goodness' sakes, of course you can!' Mary-Ann intervened. 'Let the man in to dine. I'm sure he'd do better buying eats than liquor. Why, if he drinks any more of the stuff, it might kill him.'

The drunk hiccuped. 'Gotta die sometime, purdy miss.' He pulled a whiskey bottle from his coat pocket and took a swig. 'Like some?' he invited, wiping his sleeve over the bottle top and holding it out to her. Close up, he looked even more fuddled, and he was decidedly unwashed and smelly.

She ignored the proffered bottle.

The clerk swallowed nervously, not knowing how to act. Mary-Ann could see his mind working. Management were going to be displeased either way. If he let the hobo in, they'd be unhappy. But if he denied the caprice of this very pert, very smart young lady, it might offend her father whom he knew was the town's distinguished visitor and the hotel's most important guest, Huey J. Charters, millionaire.

Mary-Ann started to relax as she saw he was going to relent, humour her, and allow the drunk entry.

'Very well then,' he said. 'But mind, Mr Carbone: there'll be no fuss and no noise.'

'Maybe you could help him to a table,' Mary-Ann said.

The clerk summoned the waiter and together the pair shepherded the man called Carbone toward a table in a dark corner of the dining-room, going as fast as his reeling gait would permit.

Carbone peeled another bill off his roll and waved it at Mary-Ann. Although his legs seemed not quite under control, his mind was clear enough for slurred speech. 'Here, missy, take a dollar fer your kindness.'

'I don't need your money,' she said.

' 'T ain't my money. Union issue, though. Part o' the four hun'erd an' thirty-two million o' war paper. Genuine greenback! Was given me by a Reb, a kindly Secesh farmer.'

'Then I'm sure I don't need it. It's probably bloodstained and stolen. My daddy's over there and he and I were vehement opponents of the Secession.'

She wanted the drunk to know she wasn't alone and that despite her sympathetic intercession, she didn't want him to become too bothersome. 'Papa's manager, Mr Gipson — he's the very big man — says all the Rebels should have been strung up from the nearest trees as soon as we'd beaten them in the war.'

Carbone reeled into the chair that was pulled out for him. Propping himself up by his elbows on the table, he filled a water glass with whiskey from his bottle and carried it to his mouth in two trembling hands. After he'd taken a long swallow, he belched and started to hum, then sing an old miners' song, beloved of the Forty-niners, in a droning, low voice.

Old Tom Moore they call me now
A relic of bygone days.
A bummer too they call me now
But what I care for praise.

Mary-Ann returned quickly and smugly to the Charters table.

Gipson snarled, not because he was disgusted but because he'd been over-ruled and bested. 'In a devil of a state, isn't he? The hotel wouldn't cater to trade like that if I were running the place. God knows what you think you're playing at, Mary-Ann.'

'Now, now,' said Huey J. Charters placatingly.

'Haven't you any compassion, Virgil Gipson?' Mary-Ann said. 'He's just an outcast of society. Look upon him in sorrow.'

She felt she'd won the round.

'You're a scamp, Mary-Ann,' her father said, with more fondness than reproof.

3

Brawl at the Mexican Café

All next day Tom Tolley felt the tension building up inside of him. Inaction sat badly on his tall, slim and wiry frame. He was like a coiled spring, pinned down, waiting for release. He didn't like what was in effect hiding in a hole in the ground when every instinct inside of him screamed out that he should be up and about, fighting for respect and his property.

He wanted to confront his enemies.

Mayor Saul Pelzer and his cat's-paw, Sheriff George Searle, were top of the list. What was their interest in the old Tolley farm? Was it just a greed for land, any land? Had their actions been spurred solely by the singular opportunity that a divided nation and war had tossed in their laps as a pretext for his

34

dispossession? Or had the people in this country really hated him for acting on his Confederate sentiment?

Tom seethed with impatience as he waited for Jed Carbone's return. He wondered what answers the old man might bring. And doubt nagged at him there, too. What if the old man didn't return? The cunning devil was a drunk for sure — you could smell it on him, see it in his eyes and sagging face. Maybe his real intention had been only to cheat him out of the money for a couple more days of whiskey drinking, and nothing more.

At nightfall, when Carbone failed to show and fulfil his promise, Tom took it as read that he'd been suckered. By first light, he was decided. He'd ride into Soldier Creek and investigate on his own behalf — to hell with the reception he might be given by Mayor Pelzer and his cronies and toadies!

The Tolley place might not be much, but it was his and he'd reclaim and restore it somehow. He recalled the old corral, big enough for about thirty head if you crowded them in, its rails nailed to deepsunk, upright posts; the pasture that had taken in nearly half the land once reclaimed from the wilderness; the small kitchen garden back of the house that had been a brave sight in his mother's lifetime; out front, the shiny pump and the trough beside it; to one side, the small but solid barn. All gone now, but not for ever, surely? They'd return, just like the warm breezes that blew at winter's end from the pines on the higher slopes to signify the coming of another spring.

By the time Tom had saddled the black gelding, mounted and gotten on to the trail, the sun was rising slowly, away on his right behind shadowed mountain peaks. He could see for miles over a vista of valley slopes, forest and foothills. The scene was alluring in its virgin wildness; so vast, big and silent a section that it awed him. He was glad he'd come home. No other country could ever call to him so loudly. He urged the horse into an easy gallop.

He was counting on at least a few of Soldier Creek's citizens remembering him kindly. He'd want to avoid going up against Sheriff Searle straight off, and would need to be circumspect.

The first place he'd go would be a café-cum-*cantina* in the town's Mexican quarter. It was run by Pedro Menéndez and his sister Carlotta. The girl was very pretty and he'd fancied her plenty when he hadn't been much more than a kid. So had all the other sprouts his age, but he knew Carlotta had held a soft spot for him. He was sure that at least she and her brother wouldn't hold a Secesh record against him. And their spicy-smelling adobe premises were just the place Carbone could have been expected to go if he was looking for cheap eats.

Tom forded the boulder-strewn river shallows where the water sparkled in the brightening sunlight. This brought him to the south end of the township.

The place had expanded in the four

years he'd been away. The main street, empty at this early hour, was now a half-mile long and boasted a new, substantial stone-built bank building among the clapboard stores, saloon, workshops and barns. The hotel looked to have grown some, too, and the front rooms on the upper floor sported ornate balconies.

On one of the balconies a party of three guests was having breakfast — two men and a pretty young woman with reddish hair that was like gold in the clear morning light.

The girl caught Tom's appreciative eye as he rode past and he felt tempted to lift and wave his hat, yet didn't. A spark of mutual interest may have jumped between them, but it wasn't part of his plan to draw attention to himself, after all.

He turned into the cross-street that led back down toward the river and the irregular rows of adobe buildings and squalid shacks that made up the Mex quarter. Outside the Menéndez café, he reined in, slipped from the saddle and hitched the black to the rail.

Pedro Menéndez didn't recognize him when he went in and seated himself at one of the free, chintz-covered tables. The swarthy, fat café owner disappeared almost at once through the arched, bead-curtained doorway to his kitchen. But Tom was pleased to find that his younger sister, Carlotta, hadn't forgotten him.

'I know your face, *amigo*,' she said, assessing him with dark and speculative eyes. 'You are a leetle older now, but you are the Tom Tolley who went away when the war came.'

Carlotta was a little older, too, Tom thought. Riper might be a better word. A mature, generously breasted, voluptuous beauty in her twenties had taken the place of the pretty young *señorita* who'd trotted about like a filly between the café tables, making hearts go pit-a-pat with her trilling laughter. But she still had the same glossy black hair drawn back from the same round face;

she still spoke from the same, even more seductively full, red lips.

'Yeah, I'm Tom sure enough, just as you're little Carlotta all grown up.'

A sadness seemed to fill her shining brown eyes. 'What are you doing here, Tom? Did you not know the Yankee court has taken your father's farm and sold it to Señor Saul Pelzer, the beeg mayor?'

'Not till two days back. That Sheriff Searle told me in no uncertain terms I wasn't welcome in these parts. But to get back to your first question, I'm also here for some breakfast. How say you ask Pedro to rustle me up two fried eggs on tortillas? Topped with some stripes of salsa and melted cheese and tomato slices. I could go for that right now. And some of your strong, hot coffee. Then maybe you could help me with the questions I got.'

The café had only three other customers, but the way Carlotta threaded through the tables took her past the one they occupied. They were loudmouthed riffraff.

It was the other side of the coin of the frontier territory's awesome wildness, which Tom had noted earlier, that it had long been the haunt of many a fiddlefoot, of men on the dodge from the law, unreformed guerrilla raiders and desperadoes of every stripe. The rejected dregs of communities closer to the mainstream of civilization. Men like these.

As Carlotta swayed by their table, one of the hardcases smirked and said something which set his companions sniggering. Carlotta tossed her head the other way, as though pointedly to ignore the bawdy comment, but one of the men caught her wrist, checking her momentarily, so that with his other hand he was able to pinch her rounded bottom through the covering thin black fabric before she freed herself and swept on, skirt swirling.

'Was she *soft*, Al?' one of the pincher's pals said, amid their dirty laughter. 'Does her ass feel as hot as it looks?'

Al grinned widely. 'I'd purely admire to git her down on all fours an' poke the pridefulness outa her, Zeke!'

Tom's gorge rose at what he'd witnessed. His face went a shade darker, but he forced himself to stay put and say nothing. After the unfair treatment heaped on himself, and being forced to sit on his hands in its aftermath, he was probably being too sensitive, too ready to leap into action. If he over-reacted at Al and Zeke's crudeness, it could only bring real trouble.

Carlotta, he knew, could look after herself. Though happy to flirt when a boy took her liking, she was an old hand at warding off unasked-for attentions.

But when Carlotta returned to fetch cutlery to Tom's table, Al got up from his and stood in the aisle. Carlotta tried to weave past him; he moved in the same direction to block her. And he put his hands on her white blouse.

'Gal, how 'bout you git offa your high hoss an' enjoy the great body you got — specially these beautiful big titties? I bet they're public property round here, truth be told.' He tugged the blouse off her shoulders, popping buttons, some through their holes, some off their threads.

Carlotta's breasts burst forth from the peeled cotton like ripe melons. The eyes of Al's sidekicks goggled; they marvelled at the full orbs with their brown aureoles and the dark nipples that leaped into stiffness at the chill of sudden exposure.

But Al got no chance to gloat over the results of his handiwork. Carlotta dropped the cutlery and slapped him hard on the face. The sound of it rang through the room like a whipcrack, and Al swayed.

'Damned uppity greaser female!' he choked and, as he regained his balance, she slapped him again. But his clawing hand caught the waistband of her skirt.

Pulling her into him, and too close to deliver a third slap, he tried to kiss her. 'C'mon, *chiquita*, act nice!'

'*Hijo de puta!*' Carlotta gasped, struggling away with such violence that her skirt tore. 'Will you have me stripped to wait table naked?'

By this time Tom was on his feet. His temper, tight as the rope that loops a maddened range steer, had at last snapped.

'Leave her be, you lousy skunk!' he gritted, grabbing Al's shoulder and swinging him round. 'If you're gonna manhandle anyone, make it a man you pick on!'

He threw a punch at Al's jaw without ado.

Al staggered backwards several yards, knocking chairs and tables awry, before his feet went out from under him and he landed heavily on his butt.

Pedro Menéndez rushed in through the bead curtain, flourishing a frying pan. But he was stopped in his tracks by the third hardcase who pulled an old but deadly-looking Walker Colt on him.

'Stay out of it, greaseball,' the hardcase said, 'or I'll perforate your fat gut!'

Al clambered up from the floor and charged, fists swinging wildly, with a roar like a bull.

Tom was amazed at his quick recovery. He ducked the first two swings, but caught a third which opened the skin over his cheekbone. Head lowered, he pummelled Al's belly, his fists going like pistons. But Al was as hard as he looked and Tom was driven back.

More furniture was skittled till Tom tripped on a chair leg and went down with Al on top of him, trying to gouge his eyes.

Tom rolled clear, but Al was up instantly and driving a boot at his ribs. Tom grabbed the foot and twisted it sharply. Al screamed with pain and crashed over. Tom regained his own feet, but immediately dived on top of Al. He seized the roughneck's shirt front at the throat and pounded his head on the hard-packed dirt floor.

After Al had taken three solid thumps, he managed to get Tom to relinquish his hold by driving a knee into his crotch.

Tom doubled over on his knees in agony.

Al jumped up with an exultant cry. His busybody opponent was at his mercy, and he was in the mood to show none. Not even to the sexy Mexican waitress whom he was going to sort out afterwards — but good.

It was Carlotta, however, who took the next and decisive move against Al's progress toward stomping the agonized Tom senseless. Momentarily ignored by Zeke, who'd been keeping a watchful, lustful eye on her but was now agog to see the interfering bumpkin get his comeuppance, Carlotta picked up a heavy coffee pot that sat on a side table by the exit to the kitchen.

Lifting it high, she rushed back into Zeke's sightlines. But it was too late for him to stop her as she slammed the pot down on Al's head, knocking him to the floor cold while drenching him with the scalding contents.

Outside the café, the quarter's excitable residents were gathering in bunches in the street, craning their necks to see in and creating a spreading ruckus. Some, who saw the gun trained on Pedro, thought the Anglos must be staging a hold-up and went screaming for the gringo law.

Tom, recovering somewhat from Al's cruel kneeing, rushed at Zeke who was attending to his stricken pal, jaw dropped.

'Get outa here, you bastard!' Tom said, taking his arm in a lock. He heaved him up and dragged him toward the door.

'What about him she's beaned?' Zeke bleated.

'I'll throw your pal out after you!'

But the third hardcase swung his Walker pistol from Pedro and fired. The slug whistled over Tom and Zeke's heads and out the door. 'That's jest a warnin', farm boy. Let him go!'

'Don't shoot no more, Wyatt!' Zeke screamed. 'Can't yuh see, yuh idjut? He's usin' me as a shield.'

Shooting wasn't Wyatt's only mistake. Pedro, freed from the fear that had paralysed him while he'd stared down the Walker's muzzle, ducked back into his kitchen, but reappeared in an instant pointing a shotgun.

'Go, you feelth! Go!'

The scattergun settled it in the two conscious hardcases' minds. Before the irate fat Mex could blast smoke and flame and a load of flesh-mangling pellets, Zeke and Wyatt were out the door. All thoughts of Al's plight and the implied promise of a roll with the excitingly endowed café wench were banished.

In the dusty street, they were met by three newcomers of their own race. Two were armed with drawn six-guns and wore tin badges: Sheriff George Searle and a bovine kid deputy, whose fair hair and skin declared Swedish ancestry.

The third, middle-aged man was dressed in a black broadcloth suit with long coat tails and wide lapels. A thick gold watch-chain stretched across his braided vest. He had a stocky build, but was of below-average height. His hatless head was topped with hair that was thinning, oiled and possibly dyed to darken it.

When Tom emerged from the adobe, dragging Al by the heels, he appeared to be in charge. 'Arrest these men! Find out what's going on here and restore the peace, George,' he said in a highpitched, clipped voice.

'Why, sure thing, Saul,' the sheriff said.

So this was Mayor Saul Pelzer, Tom thought. He had the flabby-fowled, pallid look of a man who spent overmuch time in closed rooms, poring over accounts. But his was the power that ruled Soldier Creek. And it didn't look like that of a smarmy politician, out to win votes with smiles; he'd employ more aggressive means to achieve his ambitions. Snake coldness clung to the man.

Searle's eyes settled on Tom's bleeding face. 'Jesus an' Mary! You're that Tolley farm boy. Didn't I tell you to ride out, Reb?'

'You did, Sheriff, but I'm here now anyways,' Tom said. 'And just as well if this is the kind of trash you let roam your fine Unionist town, molesting innocent womenfolk.'

Pelzer's ears pricked up at the exchange. 'Did I hear correctly, George? Is this the ex-Confederate Tolley? Here in town just when we're being checked out by the great Huey J. Charters!'

Searle shuffled his feet and tried to square his rounded shoulders. ' 'Fraid it is, Saul. Thought I'd scared him off day afore yesterday. Seems like he's more dumb than it'd be reasonable to figure.'

'Shit!' Pelzer spat, lowering his high voice. 'The idea was to get rid of the kid if he showed, not have him round hunting trouble. And certainly not now. Looks like you made a mess of your scaring-off, Sheriff.'

The mayor of Soldier Creek was seething with annoyance. 'Get him out of sight — lock him in your jail!'

4

Under Arrest

'Hey,' Tom interjected. 'That ain't right. It was these other jaspers that were hunting trouble, not me. They assaulted Carlotta Menéndez in her café. You got no call to lock me up.'

'Shut your trap, Tolley!' Searle said. 'You're gonna face charges in court.'

'What charges?'

Pelzer snapped, 'Brawling in a public place.'

'I weren't brawling.'

'Then who knocked this man unconscious?' Pelzer asked, gesturing at Al, prone in the street and crouched over by his disconcerted sidekicks.

'Me,' Tom said. 'I was defending a lady's honour.'

The two lawmen took hold of him and escorted him away from the café,

52

heading into the main street and to the sheriff's office and jail.

'Ask Carlotta and Pedro to tell you what happened,' Tom pleaded. 'They'll back me up.'

'Save your protests for the circuit judge — when he shows,' Searle said.

Tom tried to shrug off the hands clutching his arms, turning and looking back at his former opponents. 'What about them? Aren't you going to arrest them?'

'On a Reb's say-so?' Searle chuckled. ' 'Sides, they're more sinned ag'inst than sinning, I'd say.'

'You're plumb crazy, mister. Why, one of 'em fired a gun, and I ain't even heeled. You know that. You took my guns off me, high-handed, with no cause.'

The noisy argument continued all along main street.

Tom observed that Pelzer trailed behind some, trying to preserve an aloof dignity. But when he, the mayor, saw that the two men and the pretty girl on the hotel balcony were witnessing the heated exchange on the street below, he purely bristled.

'Quit your yammering, will you, you fools?' he hissed. 'That's Huey J. Charters, the millionaire, up there. I want him investing in this country. It isn't going to happen if he thinks this burg is some kind of ruffians' hell-hole.'

* * *

Across the breakfast-table Virgil Gipson wolfed eggs and steak, and Mary-Ann found the spectacle disgusting.

Steak again. She was eating her own eggs scrambled, though they weren't of quite the fluffy texture she would have liked. Couldn't this two-bit hotel back of nowhere find a nice slice of ham for a change? Not that it would improve Gipson's eating manners.

Really, this whole expedition was becoming the most dreadful bore, though it had been fun teasing Gipson with the old drunk called Carbone the night before. And just ten minutes earlier she'd finally seen, riding by, an apparent inhabitant of this godforsaken dump who'd looked human and interesting.

He'd worn a faded grey topcoat with darker patches that might have marked the places where once badges and insignia had been. His shoes, she'd noticed, were more like low-heeled cordovan army boots than the kind of footwear the riders and farmers hereabouts wore. But his black horse was well cared for. Moreover, he'd had the tall, slim build she thought a prerequisite to handsomeness, and when he'd looked up to the balcony — aware of her as she was of him — she'd looked straight into the kind of eyes that had seen danger and faced it through.

How intriguing! That old grey coat. Could he be a defeated Rebel soldier down on his luck? She hoped that if he was, he'd have changed his political views. She, like her father, had no time for Secessionist nonsense.

At this moment, buttered toast and a newspaper were competing for Pa's attentions. The paper, the *Weekly Arizonian* and days old though newly delivered from Tucson, won the battle. He shook off the crumbs and addressed her in the booming voice he was inclined to use when especially satisfied.

'Look, my love, the paper has word of our travels into the territory. The reporter makes me sound quite famous.'

He brushed more crumbs from his sandy moustache with a napkin and handed her the sheet.

'Of course you're famous, Daddy,' she said, amused that he'd never quite gotten used to celebrity as a self-made millionaire. She scanned through the report: Kentucky-born; went as a young man to work in the lead mines at Galena, Illinois. Came West in a wagon train; fought Apaches; worked like a Trojan to build a cattle-raising business. Created the beginnings of an empire by selling beeves to the military during the Mexican War. Invested shrewdly post '48 in railroads, freighting, banks and — most importantly — mining . . .

She drank in the facts re Huey J. Charters that she knew so well, but decided her daddy's ego needed no more massaging. 'Ah, how fascinating!' she cried with mock delight, picking on another item. 'An enterprising showman is exhibiting a company of trained fleas in the cities of the Atlantic States. And to crowded houses. It says their feats as described in the Eastern papers are truly surprising.'

Gipson snorted. 'Must you josh about everything, my girl?'

'I'm not your girl, Mr Gipson.'

Her father clapped his hands. 'Come now! Can't you two make an effort to get along together? The paper is estimable in all its reports, I'm sure.'

'Of course,' Gipson said agreeably, 'though it has a dark side to it. Didn't the feller who bought it in '59 shift its publishing from Tubac to Tucson after failing to kill its editor in a duel?'

Trust Gipson to know something like that, Mary-Ann thought. But it was almost as he mentioned the word duel that a gunshot rang out not far off, as though to confirm that rugged times and events still prevailed in these frontier places. Putting aside her attempt to frame a pithy retort, she dropped the newspaper, stood up and looked out over the balcony.

Townsfolk were craning their necks from windows and gathering on the street. Among them was Jed Carbone, emerging from the alley that led to the back of the hotel. From the scraps of garbage clinging to his coat, Mary-Ann guessed he'd likely dossed down among the trash barrels there after his drinking excesses of the night before.

Then, from the cross street, came the knot of struggling, yelling figures that was the centre of the attention. Two were peace officers, wearing badges. Behind them, just about hopping from foot to foot, was Saul Pelzer, the man who'd introduced himself to her father on their arrival in Soldier Creek as the town's mayor. But it was the lawmen's prisoner who brought the gasp to Mary-Ann's lips.

It was the young fellow who'd ridden by on the black horse, his face now bloody. She tried to tell herself she was merely curious. Yet he was as good-looking as she'd thought when he'd first passed by. In point of fact, he was strikingly handsome, she quickly decided. And now, surrounded by adversaries, he seemed even more alone.

'Oh, the poor boy,' she said. 'They're dragging him along like a sack of corn! What can he have done?'

The sheriff kneed the prisoner in the back. 'Keep going, farm boy! It's the lock-up for you. We can't have a Reb breaking the peace this way.'

'Breaking the peace! You've got a gall, Sheriff,' the captive said.

There was more altercation of the same kind, but Mary-Ann was baffled by it. 'What in heaven's name is going on down there?'

Gipson figured it out the fastest. 'Seems like the kid is an ex-Confederate who's been making trouble. That shot we heard was part of the ruckus, I guess. Well I hope he gets what's coming to him. Hell, these unreconstructed types make me mad. Not a penny to their names and they think they can do as they like. Nation-loving folks have a duty to take 'em down a peg.'

'Maybe even lynch them?' Mary-Ann asked sarcastically.

'You know our — your pa's — feelings on the issue, Mary-Ann dear. They'll ruin a good land. A necktie party mightn't be a bad idea at that.'

The colour blanched from her face. Daddy could be cranky, even ruthless, but Mary-Ann didn't think he'd advocate hanging for the farm boy being marched to the hoosegow. She certainly didn't. He was far too handsome a bravo. She didn't want him dancing on the end of a rope with his head in a noose. She wanted him cleaned up and dancing with herself.

Her playful nature reasserted itself and her mind ran ahead, speculating on the chances for a little more funning. It would be at the expense of the self-important nobodies who ran this boring, one-horse town, and it would bring her into contact with the attractive ex-Reb prisoner. All at the one and same blow, Virgil Gipson would be put out, too. His crude, supposedly amorous plays were getting tiresome and anything that disconcerted him would be a delight.

The chance for Mary-Ann to firm up and put her vague plans into action came within the hour.

Mayor Saul Pelzer bustled into her father's upper-floor front room. To Mary-Ann, he was plainly seeking to further ingratiate himself. He had with him a large package, wrapped in oilskin and addressed to her father at the hotel.

'I thought I'd deliver it myself,' he piped, jowls trembling. 'It just came in the Overland Mail and I'm the local agent, owner of the Soldier Creek station.'

And every other second thing in town, Mary-Ann thought he might have added. But he had other concerns on his mind, and he revealed what they were, and his real motive for visiting, when he rushed on to explain away the street disturbance earlier.

'Just a young varmint flexing his muscles, so to speak. Fought for the Confederacy in the war, so you can figure his state of mind for your ownselves, I'm sure.'

Mary-Ann's pa harrumphed noncommittally. He turned the package Pelzer had brought this way and that before taking a jack-knife to the wax-sealed ties and waterproof wrapping.

'It's from North San Juan,' he told Gipson, naming the small but substantial town in California where he had an office and hydraulic operations for mining gold.

'Ah, sure,' Gipson said. 'That'll be them forwarding those samples of the new inventions from the Swedish feller — the chemist Alfred Nobel.'

'You're right as always, Virgil.' Charters spread the oilskin on the table and set out the contents. 'See, Mr Pelzer? Here's detonating charges and percussion caps of the type patented just last year. Our company is right up with the latest, you know.'

The men were soon engrossed. But as far as Mary-Ann was concerned, their new toys were just another bore. Unnoticed, she took her chance and slipped from the room.

The imp of mischief danced in her blue eyes.

5

Gunplay at the Lock-Up

Mary-Ann found Jed Carbone still apparently dozing off the effects of his spree. This time he wasn't among the hotel's trash barrels but on a lice-infested hay bale back of the Pelzer livery stable.

'Do you remember me, Mr Carbone?' she asked.

'Why, indeed I do, missy, an' howdy. Yuh're the purdy li'le lady who got them dam'blasted, ornery hotel coyotes t' lemme eat their fancy grub.'

'That's right. You thanked me for my kindness and offered me money, which I refused. But I've found another way you can repay me. By doing me a little favour. Are you willing?'

Jed scratched his armpit thoughtfully. 'Waal, awright, mebbe. I weren't

64

expectin' this a-tall. Say your piece an' lemme think on it.'

'Have you seen the lock-up back of the sheriff's office?'

'Sure. I bin aroun' this town a week or three, but they ain't gotten me inside it yet.' He cackled. 'An' I don't cotton to hornin' in thar neither. Hotels, yep; jails, naw!'

Mary-Ann gave him a winning smile. 'You won't have to go inside the jail. I aim to do that part.'

'Yuh do? What fer?'

'I'm going to free that young man they locked up this morning. Now listen very carefully . . . '

After she'd given Jed Carbone his instructions, which he agreed he could carry out, she equipped him with a box of lucifers bought at the mercantile. That part of her preparations was then as complete as she could make it. She had a gnawing doubt that the old hobo had it all straight in a mind which must be blurred by drink, but it was the best to be done with the help at hand and worth a try, surely?

Next, she looked for a child. The first she saw was bowling a hoop and she decided against approaching him. But the second was a lively small boy carrying a home-made fish-pole and headed for the river. 'Ideal!' she purred, and stopped him.

Young as he was she felt confident when she spoke to him that he could play his role in the affair as well as Jed Carbone. His eyes widened eagerly when she showed him the old gold eagle coin that would be his reward. 'It's worth ten times a silver dollar,' she told him.

The grubby boy was so impressed, she wondered whether she might not have overplayed her hand. She was so ignorant of money matters, having always lived with a surplus of the stuff. Maybe a quarter would have served as well, if not better. She didn't want the boy blabbing the story of his good fortune before he'd earned it. But straight off he ran toward the river to do her bidding.

Mary-Ann took a deep, steadying breath and hurried the other way, to the sheriff's office.

★ ★ ★

Tom Tolley sat on the wooden bunk under the barred window set into the thick stone wall at the back of the cell. Jail was a new experience for him. He hoped it would be short, but given the attitude of Sheriff Searle and Mayor Pelzer he had grave misgivings about the likelihood of that.

Too, there was the inscription carved on the bunk — he presumed laboriously by a previous occupant of a religious if not wholly penitent persuasion. The wood was hard and it must have taken more than a day or two. It was a Biblical text that ran: 'The Lord despiseth not his prisoners. Psalm 69.'

Tom felt like he was in a cage. But through the cell front of floor-to-ceiling iron bars he could see most of the sheriff's office. This because the door leading to the three-cell block had been left open, presumably for ventilation, since the sheriff, who took his ease in a cushion-padded wooden armchair with his feet on a battered desk, seemed to have an office habit of smoking fat, evil-smelling cigars. Even now he reached into his pocket for another, bit off the end and lighted it.

The office filled with the foul smoke which drifted down the passage to Tom's cell. In the office, the young deputy started to cough.

'What's the matter, Nancy?' leered Searle. 'Feeling a mite poorly today, are we? Mebbe it's the time of the month.' His chuckle was full of smutty mirth.

The Swedish-iooking law pup's full name was Nansen Ernst, and Tom had quickly picked up that he resented the feminine nickname and the constant cruel ribbing that was his boss's sport. His fair complexion would grow bright red to the roots of his flaxen hair.

On this occasion, just as his face was returning to its normal hue, it started to colour again. The reason came into Tom's limited view. A stunningly pretty young woman was approaching the office on the trot. Tom recognized her as she rushed in. She was the redhead he'd been impressed by when he'd spotted her on the balcony of the St James Hotel. There was plainly nothing wrong with Nansen Ernst's masculinity. He was as susceptible to her charms as Tom himself: it was merely that his flesh and blood had an unfortunate way, for him, of letting it show.

But the girl ignored the kid deputy if she noticed him at all. She came to a seemingly breathless halt in front of Searle's desk as he swung down his feet.

'Sheriff, come quickly!' she gasped. 'A little boy fishing has fallen in the river. He's drowning and no one's there to save him!'

Searle didn't hesitate. He jammed his hat on his head and complied with her summons. Tom thought, this female has some pull, for sure.

'Just stay put, Nancy, and don't let anyone near the prisoner,' the lawman flung over his shoulder.

For several moments, the girl's startling entrance had occupied all of Tom's attention. Now it impinged on his consciousness that strange noises had been coming from the adjacent cell to his right, as though some kind of debris was falling to the floor.

He began to smell burning wool, too, and cast a swift eye over the three fusty, once-red blankets heaped at one end of his bunk. No fire there. But what of the similar mouldering pile he'd seen in the neighbouring cell?

Meanwhile, the girl, left in the office with the deputy, was trying to engage him in small talk, much to his tongue-tied embarrassment.

'My name's Mary-Ann,' she opened chattily. 'Who might you be? Are you Sheriff Searle's assistant?'

'Y-yeah.' he stammered, all hot and

bothered. 'D-deputy Ernst. N-Nansen Ernst . . . '

Suddenly, Tom saw flickering on the shadowed walls of the passage and smoke that had nothing to do with Searle's obnoxious cigars.

'Hey, look!' he called. 'Fire, Deputy, fire!'

'Oh my!' Mary-Ann said. 'There is a fire, too. Quickly, Deputy, fetch some buckets of water!'

Nansen Ernst needed nothing more to make him jump to his feet and flee the office. To Tom's astonishment, Mary-Ann then dodged round behind Searle's desk and took the big ring of heavy keys from their hook by the passage to the hoosegow.

She brought the keys to his cell, found with trembling fingers the one that fitted the lock and swung open the heavy grille door.

The billows of smoke from the cell adjacent were already abating and, as Tom came out, she called into the emptiness, 'Throw some more rubbish through the bars, Mr Carbone! Use another match!'

No response came.

She said to Tom, 'I think the people who run this town are being mean to you. I've fixed this fire to give you the chance to escape. But I'm afraid the man who's helping me is a poor specimen and bungling his part. Do you need a gun? There's loads in the sheriff's office.'

Tom moved past her to Searle's gun cabinet. Among the pieces it contained, he recognized his own weapons. 'I'll take back my own .44 Colt Army,' he said. 'That ain't no theft.'

He scooped up the six-shooter and was checking its loads when the green deputy lurched in from the street with two buckets of water.

'Sh-shit!' the boy blurted. 'You ain't supposed to be up and out, no matter what.' He saw the gun in Tom's hands, dropped the water and went for his own revolver, pouched in a holster high on his hip, in a conventional draw with the right hand.

But Tom's hands moved faster. Quicker than the eye could follow, his iron was hefted and pointed. The Colt spat flame and roared.

The eyes and mouth in Ernst's scarlet face opened wide with the terrible fear of death, and there was a second roar of exploding powder as his gun was snatched from his grasp to hurtle against the office wall, causing the cocked hammer to fall on a loaded chamber.

Mary-Ann screamed. 'No, no! Stop it, both of you! Someone will get hurt.'

Ernst clutched his right wrist which had been jarred with bruising, wrenching force by the disarming slam of Tom's shot.

'*Great God Almighty, Nancy! What's going down here?*'

Searle plunged into his office, pants wet and river water slopping out of his squelchy boots. On the instant, he went for his gun, a Remington, which was lower slung than Ernst's, more in the manner of a regular shootist.

Tom seized Mary-Ann by the arm and threw another deterrent shot in the general direction of the lawmen, who hunted cover behind the desk. Pulling the girl between himself and Searle, Tom forced his way through the office and out into the street.

Shots fanned past them as Searle pursued.

They pounded down the street. More wild slugs ripped the air around them as Ernst joined the gunplay, firing left-handed.

Shocked townsfolk scattered.

Tom dropped to the scant cover of a stone water trough, put in by some public benefactor for the use of horses. But Mary-Ann wrenched free and took to her heels in the direction of the hotel.

'I'm sorry! So sorry!' she cried. 'Things have gone terribly, terribly wrong!'

Maybe her departure was for the

best, Tom thought. Searle and his deputy were unlikely to shoot her deliberately, and they had him pinned down here.

For himself to move would be unthinkable. The whole town could get caught up in a running gunfight and innocent people might die. He swore to himself, regretting his impetuosity. What had the crazy girl been thinking of, springing him like this?

She'd mentioned Jed Carbone's involvement. What was his game? He'd not reported back at the farm as he'd promised, and Tom suspected he'd squandered the money he'd entrusted him with on his pleasure, which at a guess was whiskey and more whiskey.

Carbone's treachery was very evident and completely unforgivable. Somehow, he'd gotten the pretty Mary-Ann mixed up in a scheme to retrieve the situation — Tom's incarceration — for which he was partly to blame.

A slug, ploughing the dirt to one side of the trough, reminded Tom his position was hopeless and dangerous. Another whined off the top edge of the stonework. Worse, a third burned across his left shoulder.

He'd been left with the dirty end of someone's stick for sure.

He was about to throw out his gun and call surrender when new, even more baffling factors were tossed into the equation. Regardless of stray lead, Mary-Ann was returning from the hotel at the double. She was pulling by the hand the older of the two men he'd seen her with that morning, breakfasting on the balcony.

Saul Pelzer trailed, looking vexed, in their wake.

'Daddy, order them to cease fire!' Mary-Ann said.

'Holy-moly!' her father said, shaking his sandy-haired head in despair. 'You've really hashed things up this time, little girl.'

'All right, I know. I've gotten in out of my depth. Just do something, will you, Daddy? Before someone's killed!'

It was Pelzer who asserted himself first. 'Sheriff Searle! Hold your fire, man. We can't have a shindig like this in our peaceful town. There must be some mistake.'

Pelzer plainly called the shots in Soldier Creek in every way. Even to stopping the gun kind. To Tom's relief, the shooting's shattering echoes died. Silence fell, sudden and deep.

The mayor strode forward, trying to make himself look taller, bigger, puffing up his chest so that the gold watch-chain glittered in the sunlight. 'Now, what are you up to, George?'

'The Reb broke out of the hoosegow, Saul. This here young lady has played tricks on us.'

Pelzer tried to laugh that one off, but he wasn't very good at laughing. He lacked the light, warm touch that might make it convincing from another politician. 'Aw, George, I'm sure Miss Charters meant no lasting harm. And remember, her father is a most *distinguished* visitor.'

Searle growled something unintelligible. 'Waal, lemme lock the dirty greyback scum back in his cell and mebbe we can forget it. That drunk Carbone was in on it, too. I saw him skulking back of the jail when I came in from the river. He can go in another cell. You and me've just been waiting for the chance to lock him up, ain't we?'

Huey Charters stepped in closer. 'Hold hard there, gents. If you up and jail these men on account of my daughter's silly prank, I'm sure she'll be most upset.'

'Mebbe just the Reb then,' Searle said. 'He was already in trouble, and I reckon it was more than a little innocent horseplay.'

Mary-Ann spoke up, smiling as charmingly as she knew how. 'Do you have to be so rough on the young man? A little mercy might encourage him to reform . . . '

'Why, that's a perfect idea,' Pelzer broke in before Searle could object.

'Exactly what I was thinking myself. See here, Sheriff. Turn Tolley loose this time as the town's special nod to Miss Charters' returning good sense.'

Tom could hear the insincerity in Pelzer's voice. He was bending over backwards to get in good with Mary-Ann's father. If Pelzer owned most of the town's enterprises, no doubt he would benefit more than anyone when the millionaire was persuaded to put money into the place.

Searle gave Pelzer a look that was as ponderous and deadly as one of the .50 calibre cartridges that went in his government-surplus Spencer rifle.

But Tom was more than glad to avail himself of the lucky break the ambitious mayor's scheming brought his way.

Townsfolk were already drifting back on to the street they'd rapidly quit at the outbreak of gunfire. Tom could hear some of their mutterings.

Women tutted. 'A Secessionist, they say . . . '

Men shook their heads in sham

disbelief. 'A Reb. Stubborn like the rest of 'em.'

'Can't see no use in talkin' to him . . . Was him started that ruckus in the Mex quarter.'

'Pretty uppity for a greyback.'

Tom wondered if any of them recognized him as a former local boy, the son of the farmer Tolley. If they did, they didn't want to know him.

The war was over. A dead letter. But it seemed to Tom that condemning him for his past sympathies was being used as a handy excuse by folk who opted to ignore what was happening in their town now. None of them dared risk their hides to buck the Pelzer faction.

He thought, too, about the black ashes and charred timber of his old home.

6

Carbone, Mystery Man

When Tom saw Mary-Ann withdrawing, somewhat shamefaced, with her father to the St James Hotel, he got off the street while the getting was good.

It was time to pause and lick his wounds. He went to the only refuge he thought might open its doors to him in Soldier Creek — the Menéndez café.

Carlotta was horrified at the state he was in. When he'd been dragged away by Searle and Ernst, his face had been bloody and bruised. Now the left sleeve of his coat was also blood-soaked and the shoulder ripped.

'Fetch hot water and clean rags, Pedro,' she told her brother.

Tom shrugged, then winced as a jolt of pain went through his shoulder. But he carried on to say, 'The arm ain't as bad as it looks. A slug skimmed my shoulder, but I think the bleeding's stopped already. How's yourself?'

'I am fine, Tom. The gringo peegs did not hurt me really. Just my feelings, you know? It is not a nice thing to be half-raped. I have you to thank that I was not shamed completely.'

Pedro waddled in with a basin of hot water.

Tom thought it must be a healthy sign that he was acutely aware of Carlotta's maddeningly voluptuous body as she helped him remove his shirt and began her ministrations.

She dabbed and she probed. 'There is no bone broken,' she pronounced.

'It's just a graze, a fleabite compared with what I've seen on battlefields,' he said.

As well as the raw shoulder wound, there were many bruises and his scabbed cheek from the fight with Al, Zeke and Wyatt to be cleaned. But Carlotta's supple fingers did the work gently, and Pedro produced a pungent-smelling but soothing salve, a Mexican herbal remedy formulated by their grandmother, who had been a *curandera* much respected by their people in the South Desert country. It was purported to assist the healing of all manner of injuries and the Menéndez household set much store by it.

'You look like you have been trampled in a stampede,' Carlotta said, finally bandaging his shoulder. 'Or been in a fight with the whole town.'

'I ain't got many friends hereabouts, for a fact,' Tom said. ''Sides you and Pedro, there's probably none.' He thought some, then added. 'Oh, I figure there's a couple might look kindly on me, sort of — a girl called Mary-Ann Charters and her father who're staying at the hotel.'

'But they are very reech people, Tom. It is said by my cousin who works in the St James's kitchen that the girl is a silly young thing who abuses her position to make trouble for hardworking people for nothing but fun. She is — what do you say? — the spoilt child.' Her black eyes swam, Tom presumed with sympathy for him. 'Is there no other who will help you?'

'I thought an old hobo called Jed Carbone might, but I reckon he was just fooling me to get whiskey money. When I came here this morning it was him I was looking for. You see, I'd staked him to find out about what's happened with my father's farm. He's let me down something bad. He was conniving with Mary-Ann in that jailbreak nonsense, I understand.'

Carlotta nodded thoughtfully. '*Sí*. I know the man you mean. A drunk, yet he looks a leetle like an old Christ. He dresses in rags, and most of the times he comes in here he cannot pay me and Pedro for his meals. But it is very strange, Tom . . .'

'What's strange?'

'Why, that last night I thought I see him, and it was most surprising to me, so that when I tell Pedro he say that I must be mistaken, that we must mind our own buseeness.'

Tom wondered if Carlotta knew how infuriating she could be in the way she gave out her information, almost as though she was deliberately withholding it.

'Carlotta. Tell it me straight: exactly what did you see?'

'Coming dark I put out the garbage in the alley back of the café, as always I do. Now the alley runs straight up the slope to the trash barrels behind the hotel. One can see all the way.'

She lowered her voice, as though what she had to tell was deeply confidential. 'The Carbone man is there and he is conversing very deeply with this very same reech gringo you speak of, who you think might be a friend and who is the father of the brat Mary-Ann.'

Tom was incredulous. 'The drunk? The millionaire? Talking together? Are you sure Charters wasn't just ordering him to move on after he'd disturbed him with drunken singing under his window or something?'

'No, Tom. It is not like that, I know. I do not hear the words they say, because it is too far. But it is a discussion they have, most certainly.'

Tom didn't like to argue the point. Carlotta was a fine and sensible girl — no, a young woman now, who could, if he let it happen, really grab his interest. The very sight of her ready smile and saucy body had done that when he'd been no more than a boy who didn't need to shave. Now she was in her alluring maturity, and he could discount her — what she was or did or said — in no way at all.

Yet she had to be wrong in what she thought she'd witnessed. Maybe it was even two other people she'd seen in the half-dark behind the hotel.

Still, Tom reasoned, he needed to track down Jed Carbone and demand to know what the hell the old hobo thought he was playing at. He resolved to challenge him at the same time with

Carlotta's story, to check it out.

It was a testimony to changing circumstances, however, that though he couldn't disregard Carlotta, and though he was no connoisseur of womankind, he no longer thought of her as the most beautiful thing he'd ever seen in Soldier Creek.

A picture of the smiling, redheaded Mary-Ann Charters, brat that she might be, kept returning to his mind.

★　★　★

Mary-Ann hated it whenever Virgil Gipson cornered her by herself. She'd never cared for him. He was a handsome man in his own brutal fashion, but uncouth. Without her father's presence to restrain him, he'd give full rein to his ambitious ideas, especially those that involved her and her future.

If she complained later to her father, Gipson would shrug it off with a dismissive, man-to-man chuckle. 'The dear girl is mistaken . . . She has taken what I said (or did) the wrong way entirely.' And he would make it believable, too.

Gipson was crude, rough, dominating, but oh so clever, so devious!

Huey Charters had been lured away to talk business at Mayor Pelzer's office.

Mary-Ann coloured slightly when Gipson came into her hotel room. She'd been changing out of her dress, which smelled badly of smoke from the fire she'd staged at the sheriff's office, and she was standing before the cheval-glass in only her undergarments.

'Well, really!' she said. 'I think a gentleman might knock before he enters a lady's room.'

'Aw, old friends like us need stand on no ceremony, sweetheart. The day's fast coming when we gotta throw in together. Your pa thinks the world of both of us, so it's the practical thing, ain't it? And a girl with assets like your'n needs a man to handle them.'

Gipson looked pointedly at her

skimpily covered breasts and she knew he wasn't talking about financial assets. She also remembered the day when he'd cornered her in her father's riding stables. She'd been only twelve then, young and curious, and being Mary-Ann, also of a daring disposition. She'd let him kiss her lips and thrust his big hands under her camisole to fondle her pubescent breasts.

The incident embarrassed her now, but at the time she'd failed to report it to her father, and she knew Gipson would deny it today. So long after, it would all glibly be put down to faulty memory, an over-active imagination, or just Mary-Ann's latest tease.

'You'll keep your hands off me, or I'll scream,' she said.

'Don't get your dander up with me,' Gipson said, with something like a dismissive guffaw at her affronted manner. 'You wouldn't be so standoff-ish or ready to play the violated innocent if I were that dirty Reb farm boy, now would you?'

The image that came to Mary-Ann's mind was not so much of a dirty boy as of a striking young man, lean and savage, untamed as the broken, tumbled and forested country into which they'd travelled.

Gipson laughed when her cheeks tinged again and he saw that he'd hit the mark with his sally. 'What was all that tomfoolery about down at the jail? Didn't you notice the feller's garb? A tramp. A cheap, foolhardy fire-eater. You were damned stupid to push in on it, I'd say.'

'Papa didn't seem to think so,' Mary-Ann snapped.

'Oh, I think he did. It's just that he's soft where you're concerned and you wind up with too many idle hours on your hands. The drunken bum and the greyback should both have been locked up and left to stew in their own juices. And you should've gotten a good spanking, old as you are.'

'Get out of here, Virgil Gipson. You don't own me.'

'But don't you think that I should?' Gipson returned swiftly. 'You're too headstrong, too hard for your indulgent father to control. When you're married to me, I'll take you in control — properly. You'll be treated regular to a lot more than the odd spanking.'

Mary-Ann laughed in scorn. 'It will never happen. Never!'

'Don't be too sure, dearie. Moreover, once I'm in charge of the Charters business empire, I'll make decisions that best serve its interests.'

She frowned. 'What are you referring to now?'

Gipson let a silence hang while he gloated. Then he rubbed his big, ugly hands.

'I'll let you in on a secret, Mary-Ann. That Reb farm boy is Tom Tolley. His father owned a place a few miles out of here that's come into Mayor Pelzer's hands. Gold has been found on the property, a rich discovery. But neither Pelzer nor the Tolley kid know that. Leastways, not for sure as your pa does.

In my opinion it's best a deal is done with the present owner, Pelzer, and fast. Your pa is going to get hisself tripped up by letting that young Reb on the loose.'

Mary-Ann digested the information sullenly. 'You're arrogant and a bully, Virgil Gipson. Not only will I never marry you — next time I see Tom Tolley, I'll tell him everything, even if he is a despised Reb.'

Amusement continued to tug at Gipson's thin-lipped mouth, threatening to crack the rock-hard face that denoted his pertinacity.

'Well, that won't be today, chicken. Your pa has instructed me that you're to stay locked in your room the rest of the day as punishment for your mischief-making. I'll give you one choice — if you want amusement, I'll stay and give it you. What say you get the rest of your clothes off and we romp on that nice soft feather bed?'

Mary-Ann lost what was left of her

temper. 'Get out of my room, you bastard!'

★ ★ ★

Tom Tolley had spent fruitless hours in Soldier Creek. Jed Carbone was nowhere to be found.

Most no one was willing to give Tom the time of day, so every enquiry he made inevitably drew a blank; sometimes a sneer and an oblique reference to his war history. Folks had been primed to rowel him at every chance. The kindest among them might nod, shuffle their feet and cough nervously. At best, his concerns weren't their business and they were keeping out of any fight.

Carbone was conspicuously absent from his customary haunts among the trash barrels back of the hotel and the rejected, manure-spoiled hay bales at the livery, where Tom did find his black gelding and a waiting bill.

The shoulder wound was starting to

nag Tom, too, as the healing process, accelerated by the *curandera*'s salve, caused its edges to knit and pull the surrounding skin and muscle tighter. It was full dark, and he was wondering about the propriety of returning to Carlotta's place and requesting a billet for the night when the wearying search produced its first glimmer of success.

Hitched to a rail outside a barber shop across the street from the St James Hotel stood Jed Carbone's burro. Martha looked about, disdainful and petulant, long ears flicking, as though she'd been left there a good part of the day, though Tom knew he'd passed the spot not more than a half-hour back.

The barber shop appeared dark and empty, it being after business hours. Then, as Tom headed over to investigate, he heard a muffled boom.

The explosion reverberated off the buildings to either side of him, but the tinkle of falling glass from behind made him swing to face the hotel.

A lazy drift of smoke coiled from an

upper-floor room with smashed windows. The room was the one with the balcony where he'd seen Mary-Ann and her father breakfasting that morning.

Tom ran.

He was one of the first to scramble up the stairs. The rest were the shaken hotel manager and those of his staff not too stunned to respond to the unexpected emergency of the blast.

They reached a landing and an upstairs hall. A flimsy-looking door hung open, splintered from its hinges. When the others halted, afraid to venture further, Tom shoved past them.

But he wasn't the first to reach the room. Charters' big, ugly companion was there. And Mary-Ann sat on the floor by the broken door, legs drawn up, face to her knees, as though she was trying to disappear within her own self, sobbing.

Huey J. Charters lay on his back on the bed, the centre and source of a room-wide spatter of sanguine human debris. About his broken head was a spreading pool of red.

An acrid, smoky smell, similar to cordite, lingered. But overpowering it by the moment was the sickly stench of bloody death.

'Get a doctor!' barked the ugly man.

'I don't think he'd be able to do any good,' Tom said.

'Not for him, you fool. For her.'

The man jabbed a thumb at where the dead man's daughter rocked and swayed in the distant depths of her mind-blowing distress.

7

Horrific Death

The Soldier Creek sawbones examined the corpse's horrific head injuries and shook his own head sadly.

Mary-Ann had rejected his attentions, and even more strongly those of Charters' burly and aggressive associate, whose name was Virgil Gipson. She'd accepted instead the comforting arms and bosom of the motherly hotel cook. But she'd refused to leave the room.

The sawbones said, 'A gruesome business. From what's left, I'd say the roof of his mouth was blown out in the explosion and the lower jaw absolutely shattered. However, I can say it was not a gunshot that did the damage.'

He replaced instruments in his black

bag and snapped it shut. He was a little, bald-headed man, shorter even than Mayor Pelzer, but he had strong-looking hands and a knowledgeable manner.

Tom was surprised that the doctor could, from his examination, reach so detailed a conclusion. To Tom, Charters' face was an unidentifiable mess that said only that he'd died a quick and violent death. Not a gunshot? Tom was bemused by the tragedy into which he'd so suddenly been thrown. 'Then what the blazes . . . ?'

Gipson intervened, curt, brisk. 'The answer's here, gentlemen.'

He gestured toward an oilskin spread on the floor beside a washstand on which stood a porcelain pitcher and bowl and a now incongruously neat pile of fresh towels.

'Mr Charters had received a package from Sweden of new explosive materials — mixed nitroglycerine and gunpowder, patented detonating charges and percussion caps that could be used as primers to trigger a controlled explosion.'

George Searle, as sheriff, and Saul Pelzer, ever the busybody mayor, had by now invited themselves to join the small party that occupied the room.

'You mean there's been some kind of accident here?' Searle asked.

The doctor scoffed. 'I think not. To judge by the evidence, the fatal explosion took place within the cavity of the victim's mouth.'

'That sounds like suicide,' said Pelzer. 'Yet I was speaking with Mr Charters only today about the high hopes we had for a business relationship.'

Meantime, Gipson made a show of moving about the items on the open oilskin with a booted toe and counting. 'At least one percussion cap is missing. I suspect Mr Charters must have put it in his mouth and lit the fuse.'

'Good God!' Pelzer said. 'Why should he do that?'

'He was drinking heavily at dinner,'

Gipson replied. 'And on reflection I can report that he has been in a despondent state for weeks. Frankly, he's had a bellyful of certain things, and his condition may have been exacerbated today.'

Searle rubbed a hand across his smudgy moustache and straightened his round shoulders. 'Ah . . . I hear you, Mr Gipson. You're talking about what happened at the jailhouse, I guess. An unpleasant incident at best, a gunfight and all, but I didn't realize Mr Charters was that put out.'

'I ain't a man who minces words, Sheriff. It's a damn shame, but to put it exactly and not wanting to speak ill of the dead, Mr Charters had a bit of a problem with his daughter's waywardness. She tested him real hard today, as you gents rightly know. A kind of last straw. It's maybe no wonder he took his life.'

Tom listened to the explanation with a new class of horror. How could Gipson speak so bluntly in the newly bereaved girl's hearing? And if the jailbreak was part of the motive for this gruesome death, did he, Tom, share the guilt?

He knew he had to say something but he was momentarily struck speechless. To his surprise, and everyone else's he guessed, Gipson got a reaction from the least expected quarter.

It was Mary-Ann, distraught though she was, who stormed at him with an angry retort to his cruel accusation.

'That is perfidious bullcrap, Virgil Gipson! My father would never have taken his own life; he wasn't like that. He was murdered!'

Tom had learned during the war that in moments of stress the human mind often displayed amazing powers of recovery. People coped with the most horrific of tragedies, seemingly for no better reason than that they had to or totally lose their sanity and their lives.

Clearly, Mary-Ann wasn't yet capable of analysing her thoughts. She didn't understand her own feelings, was probably all mixed up. But the essential sand and sassiness in her makeup was carrying her through. Tom saw her character in a new and better light. Surely there was more to this millionaire's child than spoiled brat.

'Mary-Ann, my dear,' Gipson said, 'you're making a baseless allegation. You're distressed. Of course you are. Why don't you go to your own room and lie down? I'm sure the medico here will give you something to help you sleep and recover your reason.'

'There's nothing wrong with my reason, you bastard, Gipson! Daddy was killed, I tell you. Someone must have put that awful Swedish thing in his mouth while he was sleeping. He always slept on his back, snoring, when he'd had too much to drink.'

'Maybe we should take notice of Miss Charters,' Tom said, a mite tentatively.

'What do you know about it?' Searle sneered. 'Maybe you shouldn't be sticking your snoot in, grey-back.'

'If it's the same to you, Sheriff, my name's Tom Tolley. And just maybe I owe these Charters people a favour. Could be I want to see they get better than Yankee justice.'

'Reb talk!' snapped Gipson. 'Justice in what?'

'In a case of murder.'

Pelzer strutted between the warring parties. 'But there is no murder, son. Who would have done it; for why? Mr Charters had no enemies in Soldier Creek, and you're the only stranger I see around.'

But the town did have another mysterious stranger. The drunk Tom has been hunting all day — Jed Carbone. Tom was about to remind them of the fact, and to share Carlotta's unproven story of an illogical meeting between bum and millionaire the very night before the latter's demise. But for some reason he delayed that, stilled his tongue and crossed first to the shattered window.

He looked out expecting to see

Carbone's burro standing at the hitch rail opposite the hotel, maybe the hobo himself camping out on the boardwalk under the barber shop's awning and striped pole. But Martha was gone. His heart leaped.

'Does anyone here know where Jed Carbone is?' he asked.

'That drunken tramp!' Pelzer said. 'Why should we?'

'He could be anyplace.' Searle said. 'If I'd had my way, he'd be in the lock-up right now, along with yourself, Reb.'

Tom ignored their rudeness. 'Well, when I came in here, his burro was hitched to the rail outside the barber shop across the street. It ain't there now. Maybe he knows something about this.'

Gipson showed interest. 'Why should he, kid?'

Pressed for explanation, he told them what Carlotta had said she'd seen less than twenty-four hours back. 'I haven't figured the rights of it, but that's how

104

she filled me in on it, even if it don't make a lick of sense.'

'By God!' Searle swore. 'Has that dirty old bastard turned killer? Who'd've believed it?'

'I just might,' Tom said. 'He sure ain't no man of his word. He's stolen money offa me and let Miss Charters down. What's to say he hasn't moved on to murder? Why, he could've slipped out the back way when we came in the front. He's a crafty 'un, you know. While we mill about here theorizing, he could be making good his escape.'

Gipson took up the argument. 'Then let's get after him! If it ain't suicide, I don't see no profit in cussing and discussing this all night.'

Except for the sawbones, the men rushed for the stairs.

Searle said, 'We'll form a posse. I know this country better than any hobo. He won't get far in the dark on that broken down burro an' the moon ain't risen yet.'

'Let me get my horse back from the

livery and I'll ride with you,' Tom said.

But Pelzer chipped in, objecting. 'Now see here, Tolley, there's still charges of disturbing the peace pending against you, as I understand. And there ain't no one to — uh — stand surety for you anymore.'

'Well, surely, there's Mr Gipson here — '

'Don't look to me, feller,' Gipson said. 'I know nothing about you, 'cept you somehow managed to turn Miss Charters' silly young head this morning. But she's got big troubles now, and bigger responsibilities lie ahead of her. I don't think she's in any position where she'd want to know about some fight-crazy, pretty-boy greyback.'

'Yeah,' Searle said. 'I don't want no *Reb* riding in the dark at my back.' He hauled out his Remington revolver. 'This ain't settled yet. Not by a long sight. You go back in the hoosegow, boy.'

That's Yankee gratitude for you, Tom thought, but he bit his tongue rather than put it into hasty words. At least he'd succeeded in helping Mary-Ann Charters by throwing doubt on the suicide explanation she found obnoxious. A killer was on the loose and it was an honest man's duty to put the law on the trail of the crook who looked like the number-one suspect.

After her outburst, however, Mary-Ann had lapsed into a silence that was frightening.

* * *

Mary-Ann fought her despair like it was dangerous river rapids into which she'd fallen or, more ominously, been thrown. She couldn't afford not to fight. She knew that if she gave in, she would be swept away. She'd be battered on the hard rocks blocking her safe passage and she would drown.

Grief could be postponed, she resolved. It had to be. Else she would die.

Her first fear was of Virgil Gipson.

There would be no stopping her father's erstwhile lieutenant now. Luckily, the turn of events precipitated by the handsome ex-Rebel's keen eyes and listening ears had obliged Gipson to join the hunt for the poor old man, Jed Carbone. But he'd be sure to return and, in the ensuing days of mourning and turmoil, he'd inflict his beastly attentions upon her.

She was not much more than a mere girl, and she feared Gipson the mines manager would know all kinds of coercive ways — legal and illegal — to overcome any resistance she might mount till he owned her and all the Charters properties lock, stock and barrel. The world was still a man's world, especially in the American West.

What she needed was an ally. A strong, brave man. A champion willing to fight her cause.

Ironically enough, fate had chosen this same fraught juncture in her life to throw up the likeliest of candidates. Tom Tolley. True, he was a Rebel, but it seemed he'd professed himself ready to put the late war behind him and make a fresh start if only others would allow it.

But Tolley had been marched off to the jailhouse before the posse had mounted up and clattered out of town lickety-split in pursuit of the hapless Jed Carbone. Could she free him yet again, and this time completely unaided?

She thought of the one deputy Searle had left behind on guard at the Soldier Creek law office. The youngest and greenest. The very same Nansen Ernst she'd already met.

Yes, she decided. If she could pull her tattered emotions together, she might manage it . . .

* * *

The trio of hardcases, Al, Zeke and Wyatt, had spent a less eventful day than Tom Tolley after their fight with him at the Menéndez café. Nightfall found them on the outskirts of Soldier Creek bivouacked behind a clump of trees that gave good cover from the stage road.

Al Jones was hurt. Not so much physically, though he had his many bruises, but in his pride. The Mex café wench had gotten off scot-free with slapping his face, hitting him over the head, and dousing him with hot coffee.

All he'd had in exchange was a fleeting glimpse of big brown tits and a tantalizing pinch of generous, shapely ass. It wouldn't do. Not by half.

A pale quarter of moon was lifting over the tree-tops in a cloudy sky, illuminating their brushy hollow and casting black shadows of the taller, solid growth. Zeke threw more sticks on to their small fire and blue woodsmoke rose into the pine-scented night air.

'It's gonna be a cold night, boys.' he said. 'Pity we ain't got that curvy Messican piece to keep us warm, eh, Al?'

Al didn't like to be reminded. 'No call fer yuh to tell me, Zeke. But mebbe we can set it to rights yet. I jus' gotta think it out, is all.'

'Don't see how that could be done nohow,' Wyatt mumbled. 'We c'n hardly git at the bitch, she livin' in a town chock-full o' hot male folk who'd be on our tails direc'ly. Yuh saw how it was with thet Reb boy.'

None of them were great conversationalists and a moody silence set in.

Soon, logs were crackling and boiling liquid in a blackened pot settled into a steady bubble. A rich smell of strong coffee did little to stir their interest, however. It took an approaching drum of many hoofs to do that.

They squirmed Indian-style on their bellies to the edge of the road to watch the long line of riders from Soldier Creek gallop past.

'A posse,' Al said. 'That sheriff an' most ev'ry able-bodied man the town c'n raise, even the mayor.'

'Waal, they ain't after us,' Zeke said. 'We didn't git a chance to do nothin' we had a hankerin' to do.'

Al's eyes lit. 'Yeah, but we got one

111

now, ain't we? Boys, we're gonna go snatch ourselves what we're purely itchin' fer — that provokin' Mex woman!'

With one thought in mind — the capture and rape of Carlotta Menéndez come hell or high water — they broke camp, such as it was, rounded up their hobbled mounts, threw on blankets and saddles and spurred off into the night.

*   *   *

Light was poor in the Mexican quarter of the nigh-deserted town, but the adobe Menéndez establishment was easy to locate. The hardcases went round the back where Al struck a lucifer and tossed it into a neat stack of used packing cases, some of which contained straw and paper scraps.

'Hey, Pedro!' he called. 'Git your fat ass movin' an' unlock this door. The trash out here is afire.'

It took several minutes and some

fanning of the flames before Pedro Menéndez emerged. Sleepy though he was, he was suspecting trickery of some kind and clutched his shotgun. But Wyatt and Zeke fell on him simultaneously from either side of the door and he was clubbed down.

Carlotta appeared, dressed in a flimsy nightgown. Her black eyes dilated with terror.

'Grab her!' Al rapped.

The woman screamed and turned back into the darkened interior. But the men were on her like hawks swooping on prey.

She was caught in their hot clutches. 'Let me go, you animals!' she blurted.

Al clamped a hand over her mouth. 'Now that ain't a nice thing to call old customers,' he said.

Zeke already had his hands under her clothes on the bare flesh, using her prominent breasts as handles to hold her heaving body. Wyatt flung himself at her legs, so that she'd have toppled if she hadn't been firmly grasped.

In moments, she was gagged suffocatingly with a bandanna and she stopped struggling as consciousness left her.

'Put her across my hoss an' let's git outa here,' Al said.

8

Duping the Deputy

When Mary-Ann showed up at the sheriff's office for the second time, Nansen Ernst was overcome with instant embarrassment.

'Wh-what are you doin' here? You can't come p-pullin' no more tricks. Why, what with your paw kilt an' all, I'm s-surprised at you.'

It seemed that when he wasn't intimidated by Sheriff Searle's gibing presence, the green kid deputy's tongue was less tied. But his red face had still gone several shades darker, which Mary-Ann reckoned might have been cute under less painful circumstances.

'I don't want to pull any tricks, Nancy,' she said contritely. 'Your friends do call you Nancy, don't they?'

'N-nope!' the boy squawked. 'It's

only Sheriff Searle calls me that 'cos he thinks it fun to give me a g-girlie name. I'm Nansen. N-Nansen Ernst.'

'Oh, yes . . . Nansen. That's unusual, isn't it?'

'It's S-Swedish. My ma says it means son of Nancy. And Ernst means earnest.'

'I'm sure you are. Why, you'd never trifle or jest with anyone. And that's the reason I came to ask if you'll sit with me at the hotel. You see, all the other men have gone chasing Carbone, and I'm very frightened, alone in my room. I can't sleep for thinking a murderer is abroad.' She shivered, making her slim frame wriggle deliciously. 'He might very well pick on me next. After all, I am my father's sole heir.'

Ernst looked tempted, and swallowed, because Mary-Ann at any time was a personable young lady. He also became palpably hot; she could feel the heat radiating from him in waves. If she'd wanted to seduce him, he'd have been a pushover, unless his nerve failed him completely.

'B-but I can't,' he yelped like a lost puppy. 'I've got a prisoner to guard.'

Mary-Ann hung her red-haired head in apparent distress. 'Oh!' she sobbed. 'I thought you were going to be specially kind to me. Do please come!'

'How can I?' Ernst said, moved by her emotional plea. 'It's all this T-Tolley's fault.'

Mary-Ann looked up sharply, as though hit by a bright idea. 'I know, you must bring him over to the hotel, too. You do have some of those new-fangled handcuff things in this law office, don't you?'

Handcuffs that could be adjusted to fit any size wrists, working on a radical ratchet principle, had been patented three years back by a W.V. Adams and were being turned out in great quantity.

'Uhh . . . sure,' Ernst said, beginning to follow her drift and seeing a glimmer of hope that he could follow his urges without exposing himself to more of the indignities heaped on him by Searle. 'R-right here.'

From a drawer, he took some early-model hand-cuffs stamped on the side of the bow 'patent pending'.

'Yes,' Mary-Ann said. 'That's exactly what I was thinking of and all you'll need. There's a spare bed in my hotel room. We can handcuff the prisoner to it, and I'll let you — er — sit on mine.'

She took the cell keys off their hook and placed them on the desk in front of the deputy, and it was like it was decided.

Ernst made his way down the passage to the cells, swinging the keys on their ring. Mary-Ann followed him closely. 'Now you be real c-careful, miss. This could be a mite d-dangerous if'n the prisoner p-plays up.'

He pushed the heavy key into the cell lock, then thought better before turning it. 'C-come here, Tolley, and hold out your hands together but inside the bars.'

Threading the open handcuffs through the bars, he made to clamp them round Tom's wrists. It was then that Mary-Ann, standing in back of him, deftly lifted the six-gun from the holster high on his right hip and jammed the muzzle into the back of his neck.

'Right, Deputy Nansen Ernst!' she said, heart leaping with unexpected joy. 'You be careful. Get your hands up. Step back to the office slowly, bringing the cuffs with you, and sit down in that big wooden armchair your boss uses. No hasty moves, mind.'

'What the hell are you up to now, Miss Charters?' Tom said.

'Isn't it obvious? I'm getting you out of here, again. I need you, or I need someone, and I know it's not this green kid, prettily though he blushes for me. Let yourself out of there and give me a hand to anchor him to the office.'

'Aw j-jeepers, miss!' Ernst wailed. 'How can you do this? The s-sheriff's gonna have my hide when he gets back.'

The cuffs were clicked into place.

Before they left, Mary-Ann took pity on the boy and pushed a couple of cushions behind his back in an apologetic attempt to make him comfortable. She'd noticed when she took the gun away that the iron had left a white circle impressed in the deep crimson of his neck.

★　★　★

'Yah-hee!' Zeke whooped. 'Yuh done it, Al. We got us what we went fer — we're inta the kidnappin' business.'

'Somep'n better'n *kid*nappin',' Al drawled. 'She's a whole lot of woman here, one to fill a head with notions, yuh might say.'

They were riding hard. Carlotta was draped over Al's horse in front of the saddle and still only half-conscious. 'Yeah, moan, bitch,' he said to her limp, jogged form. 'Yuh'll be needin' the practice fer plenty o' that.'

Wyatt, the one who always saw the flaws in their nefarious schemes, tugged at the reins of his horse. 'Haul up, y'all. Hell-fer-leather's gonna wind m' cayuse. We know what we're a-goin' to do, but where-abouts we ridin' to do it?'

'What about the holler where we wuz lyin' up, down under the pines?' Zeke asked.

'Hell, naw,' Al said. 'Too close to the stage road. 'Sides, Searle's posse might scour places thataway fer sign if'n they don't kitch the poor bastard they was huntin'.'

'We gotta go someplace,' Wyatt said. 'We can't keep runnin'.'

Carlotta struggled, making sounds muffled by the cruelly tight bandanna that gagged her.

Al brought the flat of a calloused hand down on her superlative rump in a ringing slap. The shudder it sent through the defenceless flesh made his mouth water. 'Hold still, woman, an' we'll make this easy on yuh, sort of. Keep buckin' an' yuh're in fer a beatin' with a quirt to boot.'

'Mebbe she wants to know where

we're takin' her,' Wyatt persisted.

'It'll take the three of us days to use up this pleasure real good,' Al said, thinking about it aloud and realizing he ought to produce an answer for Wyatt. 'Sure ain't nothin' I wanna do quick an' once in the grass. We been put to considerable risk an' bother an' we want a payoff. I know jest the place fer the payin'. An old farmhouse, not five-mile off. Burned out, but with a handy cellar where a woman can be stashed out o' sight. Thar's caves on the property, too, so it ain't a hard place to hole up.'

'I know thet place,' Zeke said. 'Right dandy fer a robbers' roost. Not too near an' not too far, if yuh know what I mean. But thar wuz an ol' hobo fossickin' aroun' it last time we passed through.'

'The hell with the hobo,' Al said. 'We'd soon fix him. Ain't nobody else gettin' a share o' this beauty. Man, she's a sight to behold.' He lifted her skimpy clothing. 'Look at it, boys.'

Carlotta made renewed argumentative sounds.

Al took a grip of her luxuriant black hair and twisted her head round. 'Shuddup! Be good an' mebbe when we've finished an' ride south, yuh mightn't be dead. We might even slip yuh across the border where yuh belong an' c'llect us a bounty from the madam at some greaser cathouse.'

He briefly studied the terrain. The moon had risen high and a distant line of peaks was silhouetted against the starry night sky north of them. Al pulled his panting horse's head around and they rode off in line at a steadier pace, heading for the nearer foothills and the timber in which nestled the Tolley farm.

* * *

Tom Tolley was far from convinced that Mary-Ann's hotel room was a better place for him to be than the Soldier Creek hoosegow.

'I'm obliged to you, Miss Charters, but this can only get me into deeper trouble,' he said.

'I don't think so,' she said, shaking her pretty red head. 'They hate you because you're a stubborn man like Rebels tend to be. Nobody else in this town is going to lift a finger to help you. I told you — I need you. And please don't 'miss' me. Call me Mary-Ann.'

Tom sighed. This was too much for him to take in.

'Look, I got in wrong with the Soldier Creek folk from the start, thanks to that pesky sheriff and the snake-smart mayor. But the fight at the café was a mistake. I want to smooth things over, find out what really happened to my father's farm, whether it was legal.'

'Ah!' Mary-Ann said, raising a triumphant finger. 'There, I might be able to help you.'

Tom was bemused. How could this girl be so feisty with her father dead and not yet in his grave?

'What do you mean and what the devil do you want with me?' he asked bluntly. 'And why do you ask me to call you Mary-Ann, like you was a friend instead of some rich heiress?'

She scoffed. 'Don't get any peculiar ideas about that, Tom Tolley. It's not your fatal fascination. In fact, I deplore your bitterness — I fear it might become a bad habit. Also, you've done some very unfriendly things to me anyway.'

'Like what?'

Her eyes flashed fire at him and she pointed her chin. 'You set the sheriff and his men after Jed Carbone. That poor old man, however unreliable, had proven himself an ally — my only one in this place — and it was ridiculous to accuse him of killing my father.'

'I don't know that I did, exactly. But you've still not answered my questions, damn it!'

She flinched, but not much. 'I need you because with my pa dead, I'm in danger from Virgil Gipson.'

'But Gipson's your pa's associate. His mines manager. His right-hand man, wasn't he?'

'Yes, he was,' she said in a smaller voice. 'Oh, this is hopeless, I guess. You'll take his side simply because he's a man.'

'I didn't say that. But surely he'd be on your side, and he'd be a bad one to quarrel with.' Tom remembered the big, powerfully built man he'd seen in the room where Mary-Ann's father had met his grisly death. 'You can see it in his eyes — the way they look at you. I've seen men like him before; hard men like iron.'

'You're perfectly right in that, Tom. He is a hard man, with ruthless ideas and ambitions. Sometimes I think he has no soul; that he was made by Satan himself in his own image. He'll try to cheat me of the Charters fortune.'

It was Tom's turn to scoff. 'You exaggerate. I think you're mebbe over-wrought, and no wonder with what's happened and all. There'll be lawyers and accountants to take care of your interests, I'm sure.'

'No, Tom, it won't be like that. Gipson won't let me have contact with them. He'll overrule them — he always does. And with Daddy gone, he'll fool himself he can bring me to his heel and force me into a travesty of a marriage. He'll get our backers and employees to tell me it's for the best, a wonderful plan for everybody and the future. Maybe it would be best for their prospects, but for me it would be sheer hell.'

Tom held his hands wide in a gesture of helplessness. 'I'm sorry, Mary-Ann, but I don't figure there's anything I can do about that. You've wasted your time, not to mention ruined my chances, by springing me out of jail.'

'I've told you why I came for you!' Mary-Ann said, exasperated. 'I'd've come if you were my worst enemy instead of just a no-account, drifting ex-Rebel.'

'What is it you want me to do in fact?'

She got back to pleading. 'I want you to get me away from this hick town, trapped by desert on the one side and mountain wilderness on the other. I'm like a fish out of water. I know if I stay here more than a few days, Gipson will find some way to work his will on me.'

Tom considered, tried to convince himself he could help her without sacrificing his own future.

'Well, I reckon you've done for my hopes in Soldier Creek anyway,' he said finally. 'The Tolley farm's lost for good, that ain't arguable.'

His resignation didn't please her. 'No. Tom, don't give up so easily. Gipson told me something about that, too — '

She was about to say more when a tapping at the door interrupted.

'Oh God!' she gasped. 'Are they back already?'

The tapping was followed by heavier, urgent raps.

The faces of all the people they wouldn't want to see flitted past Tom's mental eye — George Searle, Saul Pelzer, Virgil Gipson.

But when the door was opened to the insistent knocks, as was inevitable since it couldn't be put off for long without good reason, their alarm gave way to surprise.

The arrival was Jed Carbone.

9

Carbone's Revelations

Sheriff George Searle's posse pounded pell-mell, two by two, stirrup to stirrup, down the stage road, peering ahead into the night for a man and a burro. But eventually the darkness and the tiring of their mounts forced the riders to ease to a canter, then to slow to a faltering walk.

Finally, they reined in and sat their horses in a bunch for a council of war.

One man said to Saul Pelzer, 'We've pushed these hosses hard, Mr Mayor. There's nary a chance Carbone could have ridden so far ahead of us on this road. Not on a mangy, fly-bitten burro.'

Searle dismounted. He had sharp eyes in his hawkish face and he used them to scan the around. 'No sign a soul's passed this way anytime recent,' he agreed.

He lifted his Stetson and scratched at the back of his head. 'He prob'ly went some other way entirely.'

Virgil Gipson said, 'Of course. He couldn't have vanished off the face of the earth, or even from this part of Arizona. You do know this country, don't you, Sheriff?'

Pelzer noted his testiness. 'Why, sure he does, Mr Gipson. I'm sure we'll hunt the suspect down before morning. George, time's getting on. Have you any other ideas?'

Heaving his tall, loose-jointed frame back into the saddle, Searle said, 'There's that place of your'n, Saul. The old Tolley farm. I seen Carbone scrabbling around there a few times. Could be he didn't hit the road out at all. Could be he headed there.'

'Then we'll get over there pronto. Check it out,' Pelzer said. 'Does that suit, Mr Gipson?'

Gipson grunted. 'Sounds dandy. We

should've been smarter — cottoned to it sooner, maybe gone there first.'

Unsparingly, they nudged suffering horses back into motion and took out at a loping run for the last fork in the road and the trail to the burned homestead.

★ ★ ★

'Carbone!' Tom exclaimed. 'You of all folks! What are you doing here?'

'The sheriff's out with a posse hunting you for murder,' Mary-Ann said. She stared at him, astonished and anxious.

'I'm aware of that, young lady,' the hobo said. 'Now no more noise, please. Let me in and close the curtains. I'm fair tuckered out handling a balky burro. Shaking off Searle's galoots wasn't so difficult, but if I'm seen and have to do it again I might not be successful.'

He sank down on the edge of a hotel bed, which creaked and sagged in memory of past abuse. 'Pour me a drink, will you?'

'Mr Carbone, I'm afraid I don't keep whiskey in my — '

'Just water, Miss Charters, just water will do.'

And the thought at last struck Tom that their unexpected caller, though outwardly still the filthy town drunk with a smell to match, was a very different man from the one they knew.

Jed Carbone requesting a drink of water!

His tangled, dirt-matted hair, the tobacco-stained beard, the puffy, veined nose, the ragged claw-hammer coat . . . these things were unchanged. But his slurred speech and vacant manner were gone, replaced with crisp speech and a bright eye. He sat upright, his formerly slouched back ramrod straight.

'By all that's powerful, Carbone, there's something mighty wrong here,' he said, all cool hostility. 'I reckon you've got some explaining to do.'

'I have that, Tom Tolley. You're a good fellow and you haven't been treated right. Not even by me.'

'Then spit it out, will you?'

'My name really is Jedidiah Carbone. But beyond that, not much of what you can see is the real me.'

'Good heavens!' Mary-Ann said, her eyes wide and shining. 'Do you mean all this is just some sort of elaborate disguise?' She set a glass of water beside him and gestured vaguely from the top of his greasy locks to his out-at-toe boots.

'It is that, Miss Charters. And I hate wearing it as much as most folks hate seeing it and smelling it. But it's part of the job I guess.'

'Which is?' Tom asked.

'By profession, I'm a detective employed by the former Scotsman Allan Pinkerton who runs a foremost agency in Chicago.'

Mary-Ann started to look excited; such was her nature, Tom guessed, that she couldn't help it, however dire the circumstances.

'I've heard of Allan Pinkerton,' she

said. 'He became famous just before the war by thwarting a plot to assassinate Lincoln on the trip to Washington for his first inauguration.'

'That's very knowledgeable, Miss Charters. What you don't know, though, is that your father was one of Mr Pinkerton's richest clients. I'm here because he commissioned the agency to investigate a certain rumour that had emanated from Soldier Creek.'

'Do tell,' Tom prompted.

Carbone took a gulp of the water Mary-Ann had poured him. 'First I must explain that the Pinkerton agency recruits some of its operatives for their expertise in areas other than law enforcement. Before I became a detective, I was educated as a mining engineer at the *École des Mines* in Paris. After graduation and returning to America, I became a nomad, working all over. One month my work might take me mule-back into the wilds of Idaho, the next into sophisticated financial circles in San Francisco.

'Eventually, I specialized in mining law, but I found working in legal offices onerous and leaped at the chance when I was approached by Pinkerton to join his agency, undertaking such enquiries as involved my field. Survey work with a difference.'

Mary-Ann took in his story avidly. 'That's quite fascinating, Mr Carbone.'

Carbone chuckled. 'I suppose to a young person it must seem so.'

Tom's brain was shuttling and rearranging these new facts as fast as a high-stakes gambler his cards, trying to see the patterns of the play. Somehow, Carlotta's report of a back-alley conference between Jed Carbone and Huey J. Charters was starting to fit in. The improbable was beginning to make sense.

He also knew now what he'd missed seeing in the cellar of the razed farmhouse. It was the empty bottles that should have been the careless evidence of an alcoholic's sojourn; there just hadn't been any in sight.

'Did anyone in Soldier Creek know your true identity, Carbone?'

'Of course. Mr Charters did, but he told no one so far as I'm aware, not even his mines manager, Virgil Gipson, though I understand he told him about my findings. It was my brief to report to Mr Charters personally, in secret.'

Tom drove to the heart of the affair. 'What findings, Carbone?'

'I was hired, as I said, to check out a rumour. Shortly before his death, your father, Thomas Tolley senior, was alleged to have sent confidential word to a Californian mining man that he thought he'd found mineral wealth in a cave system on his farm — a tunnel with walls veined by rich gold and silver lodes. I came here and over several weeks, I followed my instructions, poked about in my role as an old hobo, and confirmed the presence of the strike.'

Mary-Ann broke in excitedly. 'Tom! That's what Gipson told me and I was going to tell you: that gold had been found on your old farm.'

'Yeah,' Tom said, bitterly. ''Cept it ain't my farm, is it? It belongs to that slippery snake Pelzer.'

'That might not be so,' Carbone said, shaking his head. 'Mr Charters had grave doubts about Saul Pelzer's right to be in possession of the land title, let alone any mineral rights. I have them, too. Hence, also, Mr Charters' intervention in your behalf, notwithstanding your Rebel past.'

'I s'pose this does help explain a lot of the secrecy and the mystery it's made.'

'The secrecy and my working undercover were mainly to prevent Pelzer from finding out about the find before Mr Charters could put in an offer to buy the Tolley farm purely on the basis of it being a speculation.'

While Carbone had been winding up his explanations, Mary-Ann had retreated into a thoughtful silence. Now she bit her lip with a suggestion of tears starting to form in her eyes.

'But who killed my father? And why? We're no nearer to knowing these things, are we?'

'I'm sorry to say we're not — yet,' Carbone said, compassion in his voice. 'If indeed he didn't take his own life, a murderer runs loose in this town. I'm a suspect, Tom is an escaped prisoner, so we're both fugitives from such law as exists in this place. You, Mary-Ann, may well be in danger of becoming another murder victim at the hands of the unknown.'

'That's a hell of a note!' Tom said.

'It's terrible,' Mary-Ann said. 'What do we do?'

Carbone's gaze was unfathomable within the surrounds of his disguise, but it was steady and his voice firm as he gave his verdict.

'I think we should pull out, all three of us. I'll report to my head office in Chicago, and together we'll put the whole case as we know it in the hands of the territorial authorities. We need reinforcements. With a whole town up against us, we've bitten off more than we can chew here.'

Suddenly, the flimsy door to the room crashed back against the wall, its knob dislodging chunks of paper and plaster, its thin lower panel splintering under the impact of a heavily swung boot.

'*T-too right yuh have!*'

Deputy Sheriff Nansen Ernst stood on the threshold, aiming a Colt revolver at them in a determined way that said, despite his stammer, he'd have every jot of nerve it would take to use it if they chose to argue.

'I'm s-sick of you f-folks m-makin' a jackass outa me. This time I'm gonna be a w-winner.'

He strode into the room and seized hold of Mary-Ann, putting his arm round her neck and the point of his gun to her head. 'Anyone g-gets smart an' I blow her b-brains out like her pa's.'

Carbone said quietly, so as not to agitate him, 'This will prove a mistake, Deputy.'

Ernst shook his head. 'I don't think so. N-not this time. I bin listenin' outside an' heard everythin' yuh said, P-Pinkerton clever-dick.'

Tom exchanged a look with Mary-Ann. Though her face had gone white, he could see she wasn't as scared out of her wits as she had a right to be.

'Nansen,' she wheedled. 'You wouldn't hurt me, would you? I like you really, remember?'

Blood flamed into his face. 'Th-that's a lie. You underrate me, more like. You d-didn't know the back on that chair o' Searle's was loose, did you? I b-broke free an' stepped through my arms. I got the k-key an' unlocked the cuffs with my mouth. D-didn't think o' that, did yuh?'

'Oh, how resourceful of you, Nansen!' Mary-Ann carolled. 'But if you heard what Mr Carbone had to say, you'll know we mean nobody harm.'

Tom said, 'All we want to do is leave Soldier Creek and get some proper justice. Now, c'mon, let the girl go.'

'I c-can't do that, Reb. I gotta make g-good fer lettin' you git out. Sh-she's made a fool o' me once too often. But I'm gonna t-tell Sheriff Searle an' Mr Pelzer about that gold. Thataways they'll let me offa what I got comin' fer gettin' s-suckered.'

Carbone tried laughing at him. 'You're plumb crazy, kid. There's more to this than your stupid fear of your bullying boss. Can't you see that?'

'S-sure. I'm not daft, yuh know. I heerd what yuh said. There's a big g-gold find. Pelzer an' Searle'll want that for theirselves. If'n I l-let yuh go, they'll k-kill me. But I reckon they'll give me shares if'n I c'n hold yuh here till they gets back.'

Most of the crimson had now drained from Ernst's face. He was even starting to sound bold. 'When I got g-gold I'll go someplace else they'll never call me Nancy or laugh at me ag'in.'

Tom kept staring fascinatedly at the gun he held to Mary-Ann's neck. A cold chill seemed to caress the back of his own neck and spread down his spine.

Was this what gold talk did to people's minds?

10

Moonlight and Gunsmoke

At the abandoned site of the Tolley homestead, Al Jones and his two hardcase sidekicks laid out their blankets and removed their boots, the fervour rising in them as they prepared themselves for the first sampling of the pleasures of their prize, the abducted Mexican woman Carlotta.

A fire had been lit in the base of the old stone chimney, but the men had their own, inner heat like beasts in rut. Only Carlotta shivered in the night, her teeth chattering in wordless fear. She knew what was about to happen to her and, realizing all effort to resist them was now futile, she lay in a huddle, waiting for it, cold and appalled.

One of their horses, tied in the nearby trees, whinnied.

'What's up with that damned cayuse?' Wyatt grumbled.

Zeke giggled in his excitement. 'Mebbe our hosses got a smell o' what's gonna go down here. Should've brung along a pretty mare to put 'em to.'

'Hush yuhself, Zeke!' Al rasped. 'Riders comin'.'

Carlotta, hearing his hissed warning, stirred out of her huddle, propping herself up on an elbow. Al grabbed her, stuffing a kerchief in her mouth.

'Yeah, yuh're right. I can hear hosses myself,' Zeke said, sobering suddenly. 'Least six or seven.'

Wyatt said, 'I reckon it's that stinkin' posse. They're headed here. Ain't noplace else on this trail.'

'They weren't after us afore,' Zeke complained.

'We hadn't snatched this woman then,' Al reminded him. 'Mebbe they went back to town an' headed out ag'in. We shoulda kilt the greaser cook.'

'What do we do?' Wyatt asked.

Al pointed. 'Make fer them rocks

upslope. We'll make a stand — pop 'em off, or hole up if we can. Thar's some caves handy higher up.'

'What about her?' Zeke jerked his thumb at Carlotta, inert in Al's clutch.

'We'll drag 'er up with us. Gimme a hand, will yuh?'

★   ★   ★

George Searle was a wily old lawdog. When he heard the whinny up ahead in the direction of the Tolley place, he called the posse to a halt.

'That weren't no hobo's burro I heard. It was a hoss,' he opined. 'Carbone was apt to spend time hereabouts, but it might be some other jaspers — and I don't reckon they'd be inn'cent pilgrims passin' through. This trail ain't the proper road to anywhere.'

Pelzer said importantly, 'That place is my property, George. If anyone's camping on the land, Carbone or contrariwise, they're trespassing.'

The sheriff dropped his mount's

reins to the ground and swung down from the saddle.

'I'll scout it out. I smell two things here — one's a fire burning, and the other'd be trouble.'

He detailed a deputy to take some of the men and advance on a separate path through the trees. 'Harris, Reilly . . . you others, work round what was the Tolley home lot. Get up among them rocks in back. See if we can't get these interlopers boxed in, won't you?'

Searle was tired. It had been a trying day and now, with these to-and-froings in the wan moonlight, his mood was getting ugly. What followed made it tenfold uglier.

He catfooted up the trail to the edge of what had been the destroyed house's front yard. He saw no one — only the crackling logs aflame in the fireplace of the solitary chimney. Drawing his gun, he stepped forward into the open.

'I'm a peace officer leading a posse,' he yelled. 'Come on out and show yourselves!'

Searle never heard the vicious crack of the rifle. The slug intended for his head couldn't have passed him any closer; a shrill whine deafened him and took off the best part of an earlobe. Blood sprayed over his shirt.

'Godamighty!' he cried, and threw himself flat.

Several alert possemen had seen the gunflash that had erupted from the dark cover of the overlooking rocks. They used their long guns in instant, ferocious reply, pumping shells as fast as the lever-action repeating rifles would operate. Those who had only older-style Sharps rifles and carbines joined in, doing their best.

The hidden enemies fired back, almost shot for shot.

A posseman screamed as lead hit him in the chest, jerking him high in his stirrups before he twisted convulsively and fell, dark blood jetting from his wound. He hit the ground hard — horrifyingly dead.

Another Soldier Creek man cursed

profanely as the stock of his rifle was smashed into splinters. 'These bastards ain't no hobos — more like *lobos*.'

He could have saved his breath. It was clear to each and every member of the posse that they'd come up against a pack of curly wolves. These boys were committed owlhoots who knew their business.

Searle mopped at the blood trickling down his neck with a kerchief and shuffled himself in reverse into the gully that ran beside the trail into the yard.

'Fall back!' he ordered his party. 'Ain't no monkeying with loco cur-dogs of this stripe.'

He wanted their attackers to hear him, too. He was pinning big hopes on Harris, Reilly and the others he'd sent on the detour. They'd get the bastards with their tails in a crack yet!

But the pincer movement didn't succeed. By the time Harris and company reached the place in the rocks where they thought the attackers were hunkered down, the only signs of their presence were in the form of empty shells and scrabbled footmarks in the looser dirt.

'They ain't here,' Reilly called.

'They didn't return this way,' Pelzer yelled back.

'Lay off yapping,' Searle snapped. 'They must've climbed higher. There's caves further up.'

Anger showed on the faces of the possemen as the two groups reunited. Reilly, a small homesteader from close to town, said, 'We rode out to git a murderer, didn't we? Well, we've sure found ourselves a whole bunch. Let's go on up an' settle these swines while we're out here.'

Pelzer said, 'We must have 'em pinned down. They can't ride out without horses and their mounts are in those trees. Despatching 'em gets my vote, too, George.'

'Fine,' Searle said. The wound to his ear was not life-threatening, but it was still bloody and throbbing now with pain as the initial numbing shock wore off. However, he knew it would demean him in the men's eyes if he was to back down from the job in hand. 'We keep a-going then. Foller me, but take it careful. They've ambushed us once with sniper fire. Don't give 'em the same advantage ag'in.'

On foot, they climbed the slope, dodging through bushes and small trees. When they'd come up to the nest of boulders vacated by the presumed owlhoots, Searle hesitated a second, crouching low, using the cover it gave in the uphill direction. Then, gun drawn and ready, he vaulted inside. From here, he could see the waist-high parapet of rocks that partially hid the entrance to the caves. And he thought he caught a glimpse of hat, ducking down.

Emboldened by the absence of retaliation from their quarry, more of the possemen joined him, including Virgil Gipson.

Gipson was peeved with the way matters were panning out. He always was peeved with things that didn't run according to his plans, which he regarded as second in importance only to God's — when he was giving begrudging credence to such an entity, that was.

He didn't see this deadly diversion furthering his interests one jot. It was a nuisance, a cause of delay he'd rather have done without, and damned dangerous to boot.

★ ★ ★

Mary-Ann tried offering Nansen Ernst an olive branch. Though the blood ran like ice-water in her veins, she summoned her very best smile and said to the crazed deputy holding his gun to her head, 'I underestimated you, Nansen, and I'm sorry, I truly am. Can't we still be friends, you and I? You know I'd never call you names, and I'm sure something can be worked out about this gold thing. You never know, Mr Carbone might be mistaken — '

'D-don't give me any more of your b-bullshit!' Ernst said, jabbing her under the chin and lifting her head with his revolver's gunsight. 'He's an expert, t-trained in France. I heard him say. M-make her stop telling l-lies, you two.'

Tom struggled to keep his voice under control. 'For God's sake, Mary-Ann, don't antagonize him. He won't listen to reason. He's pure loco.'

The tense stillness and silence of their standoff was restored. Mary-Ann tried to distract herself from her perilous position by trying to see artistic merit in the swirls of huge brown leaves and outsized fruit that patterned the hotel's hideous wallpaper.

★ ★ ★

Searle challenged the ambushers a second time. 'Come out! You're sitting ducks up there. Give yourselves up an' you might be spared.'

His answer was an outburst of angry cursing. The bushes off to the left of the higher outcrop of rocks trembled. Rifle barrels were shoved through.

'They're gonna make a fight of it!' Harris warned, and to a man the posse hunted their best cover. Even so, when the ambushers poured down a blistering fusillade of fire, bullets grazed one man's ribs and tore a chunk out of another's hat brim. The leaden hail fairly spanged off the rocks, the ricochets punishing them afresh with showers of stone chips and choking dust.

They retired in good order, their guns pounding a reply wherever possible, beyond the reach of stray shots.

'We ain't giving up. We gotta clean the bastards outa there, fellers,' Searle said.

'Yeah, but how?' someone asked.

'We'll fire the brush. It's dry enough. The wind and updraught will carry the flames a hundred yards in the right direction in quick time. That should settle their hash.'

Men scurried instantly to put the

plan into action. Fires began to burn in a dozen chosen spots and crackling flames zig-zagged across the ground from one dry clump of growth to another. In minutes, the abandoned Tolley place and its surrounds were lit up with a leaping orange glow that displaced the colourlessness of the moonlight.

The scene must have looked like this the night they fired the old farmhouse, Gipson thought. Somehow he couldn't imagine the destructive deed having been done by day.

The hardcases smelled the smoke blown towards them and saw what was happening. They yelled strings of profanities. One (it was Wyatt) leaped up, flinging a Henry rifle to his shoulder. But the dark, swirling smoke obscured his vision, maybe lending him a false sense of his own invisibility. Anyhow, he was shot twice before he could fix on a target of his own. One slug hit him in the shoulder, causing him to lose hold of his gun. The other ploughed through his right eye.

He gave vent to a short, frightful scream. Blood gushed from his emptied eye socket. He staggered two steps and fell on to his knees before he rolled over and was dead.

His companions tried to sneak out of the weird yellow firelight into the shadows beyond, which were the darker because of it. But the safety that beckoned them played them false. The moment they rose up to leave the cover of the boulders they were exposed to the merciless, blistering fire of the posse.

Gipson, now within handgun range, saw a figure rise that he thought was clad in a blanket and the tattered, wind-blown scraps of something white. Without pause, he shot at it through the billowing clouds of firesmoke and gunsmoke.

The slug appeared to slash the side of the figure's head, knocking it back down behind the rocks like a lightning bolt. After it was gone, Gipson wondered if he'd seen it at all, or if it had been only some trick of the light, a shift of shadows in the rolling eddies of the smoke.

The two others who quit the rocks to escape the oncoming fire and the posse's roaring guns fared no better than Wyatt.

Zeke was cut down in mid-stride, his back turned to his pursuers. He flung up his arms and crashed headlong on his face. He was holed through and blood poured from his chest to soak into the parched ground, taking his misspent life with it.

Al Jones turned on his tormentors, a gun in each hand, and tried to shoot it out. But he was on his own now and the target of every posseman's gun. The blast of fire lifted him off his feet and threw him backwards. He was dead before he hit the ground so hard that his perforated, bloodied corpse bounced.

Immediately the echoes of the firing died, the mayor shouted, 'Stamp out the brush fires, men! I don't want my timber going to blazes.'

Gipson thought Pelzer a little man with a bellyful of self-importance. But the Soldier Creek men rushed to do his bidding, regardless of the fresh dangers of injury it posed. Gipson observed how the men hung on his every word. Even with the sheriff, it was a case of Pelzer's wish was his command. His was the power here. If he wanted a thing done, it was.

Gipson envied politicians who were crooked, which left few he could regard with contempt. Even pompous Pelzer came into the larger group. Gipson had gathered that a good number of the Soldier Creek citizenry were in danger of losing their property to Pelzer through foreclosure.

Sparks flew and the fire was reduced to a few hot spots smouldering obstinately among the ash.

The sweaty, blackened men, some with scorched boots and trouser legs, then moved over to examine the dead.

Gipson, who took no part in the firefighting, approached Pelzer who also stood by.

'Must be a responsibility, holding the title to a place like this,' he said. 'Mebbe it would be a good idea to unload it. Suppose I take it off your hands?'

Pelzer's complexion was ghastly in the moonlight, its office pallor accentuated and mottled with hectic splotches of fatigue. He was plainly unaccustomed to gallivanting across country by night. In fact, he likely avoided the outdoors as much as he could. Gipson was positive his butt had never been calloused by long hours in the saddle.

The mayor eyed Gipson suspiciously. 'I don't know that the farm's for sale,' he said.

'Aww . . . anything's for sale if the price is right. I could offer you Charters money right on the barrelhead.'

'We'll talk about it in the morning then, back in town.'

Gipson said no more but mentally he rubbed his hands. The mayor didn't entirely trust him, but did he anyone?

Moreover, Pelzer would be looking, as such men did, for the quick, easy way to an easy life. Gipson thought it should be within his capabilities to dress up Charters's death as a possible threat to doing business if it was left any later. Offer him a tempting, instant cash deal and he'd be in with a chance to make a killing.

The sheriff and the possemen were going slowly from body to body, making a grisly examination of the carnage.

Pelzer said, 'Why, George. I do believe it's the three men Tolley was caught brawling with in the Mex quarter.'

' 'Deed it is, Saul,' the sheriff replied. 'Now ain't that a turn-up for the book.'

Reilly said, 'Well, they're dead sure enough. We'll have to bury 'em, I guess.'

'Naw,' Searle said. 'Why should we bother? We ain't got no digging tools along, and they were just fiddlefeet

— border trash. Leave 'em as food for the varmints.'

So the living swung on to their horses and departed the scene, hauling their dead and wounded with them down the trail toward town.

And not long after the coyotes and the rats came to feast unsqueamishly on the bloodied corpses of Al, Zeke and Wyatt, badmen but not bad meat.

11

Negotiations

Tom Tolley couldn't remember being in a worse bind, not even during arduous Civil War battles. His position, sitting alongside Jed Carbone on the sagging second bed in Mary-Ann Charters's hotel room, had become cramped. He dearly wanted to move, but he dare not take the chance. If he did, the twitchy Deputy Nansen Ernst might act on his threat to blow out the pretty heiress's brains with the revolver he held behind her ear.

'I reckon the posse must've got lost,' he ventured. 'They've been gone an awful long time, Deputy. Mebbe they won't get back before sun-up. They ain't gonna find Mr Carbone, that's for sure.'

'Sh-shut your mouth!' Ernst said.

'F-fact is, I'm a right p-patient feller, so you c-can't trick me inta changin' my plan.'

Jed Carbone lifted his eyebrows. 'Ah! You have a plan, do you, Deputy?'

' 'C-course I do, but you ain't playin' no part in it, P-Pinkerton asshole. I d-don't trust you a-tall.'

Tom asked, 'Who is in this plan of yours then?'

'Y-you are, Reb. I seen the way you l-look at this two-timin' f-filly. I figure you're that s-sweet on her, you won't p-put a foot w-wrong, less'n I put a bullet in her h-head.'

Ernst started to look smug at his own cleverness. Tom thought his blond bovinity was easier to take when he was the blushing kid.

'Yeah? So what do I have to do?'

'When the p-posse rides in, you'll g-go down and fetch Sheriff Searle and Mayor Pelzer up here. J-just them t-two.' Ernst was starting to get excited again and his stammer became more pronounced. 'It ain't d-difficult. If you r-run out on me, I'll k-kill Miss Ch-Charters.'

Tom grimaced, but nodded his head. He hated to think what Searle's reaction would be when he saw his prisoner loose again on the main drag, but there was nothing to be gained in pointing out that this might be all it would take to upset the conniving deputy's apple cart.

'What do I say?' Tom asked.

'N-nothing about n-no gold. Just t-tell 'em I'm up here and y-you're still m-my prisoner.'

'Well, I guess that's pretty smart,' Tom said drily. 'After all, you don't want the whole town in on your good luck, do you?'

Carbone was unimpressed. 'Damn it, Deputy, you don't need to sell your soul this way to shake free of a rotten boss.'

Mary-Ann said, tentatively, 'I could give you enough money to ride out of here now, Nansen.'

But Ernst, even if he listened, was

adamant. 'The Reb d-does as I say, and that's f-final.'

Besides, it was too late for argument anyhow. A clatter of many hoofs growing ever louder could only signify the return of the posse.

'Get going, Reb,' Ernst jerked with nary a trace of a stammer. 'No tricks, remember, or she dies.'

Tom Tolley descended the hotel stairs. Relief at being allowed to move again was wholly negated by the knowledge that Mary-Ann's life depended on him getting this thing Ernst was making him do exactly right. He hoped, too, that Carbone realized too much was presently at stake for him to make any plays a smart detective might have up his sleeve.

The possemen were dispersing outside the sheriff's office. As luck would have it, Tom was seen by George Searle first.

'By God!' he said, stabbing a finger at him after he'd dismounted. 'I slapped your ass in jail. By whose say-so are you on the street now?'

'It was Deputy Ernst's idea, Mr Searle sir,' Tom said swiftly.

He sensed a bigger explosion would have already come had the sheriff not been bone-weary from long hours of night riding. A smell of smoke hung around the posse, too, and many of its members wore scorched clothing and nursed obvious gunshot wounds. But though that gave Tom cause to wonder, his business was too perilous to endanger with questions. He could not afford to provoke anger.

'Nancy let you out?' Searle was incredulous. 'What the hell is that ninny up to?'

'Oh, I ain't let out,' Tom said. 'I've been held prisoner in a room in the St James Hotel.'

'The hotel!' Searle roared. 'For Cris'sakes, why?'

Tom improvised. 'I guess it's because that's where he's also holding Jed Carbone.'

Saul Pelzer's drooping head lifted the

instant he heard the name. 'Carbone! D'you mean to say that while we've been chasing across the country to hell and gone, Sheriff Searle's fool deputy has arrested the killer in the hotel?'

'Something like that, sir. He — that's Deputy Ernst — says you, Mr Mayor, and the sheriff here are to follow me back to Miss Charters's room soon as you can. Just you and Mr Searle, he was most particular.'

Searle pulled a cigar out of his pocket and bit off the end, which he spat on the ground. He jabbed the cigar into his mouth, and puffed furiously to make the foul leaf take the match.

'I don't believe it,' he mumbled between smoky breaths.

Pelzer coughed. 'Well, George, maybe your young deputy has some initiative after all. We'd better scoot along and see.'

Tom drew a long breath. So far, so good. But his mind wasn't eased for more than moments.

Virgil Gipson, who unlike the others

didn't have a home awaiting him, naturally followed the party to the hotel where he had his room. Tom remembered that this man was regarded by Mary-Ann as 'Satan himself'. She wouldn't want to be delivered from Ernst's hands into his.

Tom decided anew that Gipson did indeed look as though he might be an ugly piece of work if you got on the wrong side of him. At this late night hour — or was it an early morning hour now? — the lines of irritation and implacability were chiselled cruelly deep in his rock-hard face.

'Carbone arrested, huh?' Gipson said. 'I told Miss Charters the old geezer was scum right from the start. I was surprised some to hear Tolley say he'd been seen consorting in a back alley with Mr Charters — God rest his soul — but I can believe he'd kill anyone for a grubstake, or even the price of a jolt of whiskey.'

Tom said nothing about Jed Carbone's declaration of his true identity.

What Gipson said bore out what the Pinkerton man had told him and Mary-Ann: his brief had been to report directly and only to Huey J. Charters.

He wondered how Gipson would react when he learned that the convenient murder suspect nominated by himself, Tom, could no longer be regarded as such. No doubt it would be back to the suicide theory so staunchly resisted by Mary-Ann.

The small group trooped up the stairs to Mary-Ann's room.

'Sheriff!' Mary-Ann cried. 'I insist you tell this idiot boy to take his gun off me immediately.'

'Shit, Nancy. What the blue blazes — ' Searle began, but for once he didn't finish. For his deputy found in himself the audacity to cut in. And the fantastic story he told quickly had all three newcomers — Searle, Pelzer and Gipson — agog.

Gipson was the first to recover his wits. 'A Pinkerton, huh?' It was his turn to be the man whose face was taking on a redder tinge, though nothing like the crimson that would have flooded Ernst's in a similar situation. 'I don't know that I can credit that. Mr Charters would never have wanted to make a fool of me. I reckon this tramp sees he hasn't a leg to stand on and he's lying in his teeth.'

Gipson suddenly stepped in front of Carbone, grabbed a handful of his dirty shirt front and pulled him up off the bed like he was a rag doll. With his other hand he tugged at the tobacco-yellowed beard. It promptly tore free from Carbone's face complete with his moustache and the puffy drinker's nose from above it, which looked to be moulded from some sort of wax.

'Goddamn!' Gipson said. 'An imposter after all.' He threw the elements of the disguise across the room, so great was his anger, then ripped off Carbone's stringy wig of matted hair for good measure.

'And a Pinkerton agent,' the revealed, younger Carbone insisted calmly.

Searle fingered his own moustache — which was real but looked more painted on than ever — and drew mightily on his stinking cigar. His fury was mounting. He'd been bamboozled, but good!

Only Pelzer, being the consummate crook he was, already had his eye on the main chance, grasping the significance of what this all might mean. After all, even stupid Nansen Ernst had done exactly that before him.

'Now hold on, gents, there was much more to Deputy Ernst's story — a matter of very rich mineral finds if I heard it right. Don't let's go to wrangling over who or what Carbone is. What we need to do is quietly check out his story. We must ride out to the farm pronto and Carbone must be made to show what he's discovered.'

Gipson looked furious that the possible secret of the Tolley farm was now shared at least five more ways — by Carbone, Tolley, Pelzer, Searle and Ernst. Mary-Ann he'd already told, of course, but probably only because he thought of her as his property anyhow.

Tom saw Gipson swallow as he mentally calculated how the price he'd have to pay Pelzer for the deeds to the farm must have suddenly leaped. That's if Pelzer was willing to sell at all.

Gipson looked sick but he pasted a smile on his face. 'You're right, Mr Pelzer. A quarrel among ourselves is the last thing I intend. I'm a mining expert my own self and it sounds like ore enough might exist out there for everyone of us in this room to be rich. For my own part, I'm willing to fetch along some of the new-fangled Swedish blasting powder and what-have-you. To get some samples of the ore in our possession would be a right handy thing.'

With these conciliatory words, the crisis seemed to be averted. Pelzer, Searle and Ernst nodded agreeably.

But Tom said, 'I'm not having a bar of it. That farm's still Tolley property, I swear it.'

Pelzer pulled himself up to his fullest height. 'George, get your Reb prisoner back in line, will you? Tired as we are, I suggest we head for the farm at first light — before sun-up and the town gets to moving and watching.'

Carbone shook his head, scowling. 'You're all fools. This is no way for grown, civilized men to behave. One man, Huey Charters, has already met his death in this business. Isn't that enough?'

'Someone killed my father,' Mary-Ann said. 'I'm more sure of it than ever. It wasn't Mr Carbone and it wasn't suicide. It was murder because of that gold.'

Gipson hissed, 'Shut up, Mary-Ann. You don't know what you're talking about. Let me handle this, or we'll end up with nothing.'

Ernst still had his revolver drawn. Searle and Pelzer were both toting conspicuous belt-guns. Tom knew that his, Carbone's and Mary-Ann's wishes were overruled. No question. So he held his tongue.

They would be riding out to the farm, like it or not.

But Mary-Ann was nothing if not forever feisty, despite the sad loss of her father and the subsequent ordeal at Ernst's agitated gunpoint, which had dragged on for several stomach-turning hours.

'You've no right to make a lady go out on horseback into the wilderness at this ungodly hour,' she said in prim tones. 'Why, it wouldn't be gentlemanly or even proper.'

Gipson snorted in derision. 'Aw, stow it, will you, Mary-Ann? You've been riding your father's horses like they were your playthings since you were a kid. We all go along, get it? Haven't you got those fancy boots and that neat little riding-habit somewhere in your suitcases? You know, the stuff that shows off your figure so revealingly.'

Mary-Ann was black as thunder at his taunting.

He smirked masterfully. 'Get behind

the screen here and change your clothes fast, dearie. I'm sure you wouldn't want me to give a hand with the buttons in front of company.'

12

'A Bullet in the Back?'

Tom Tolley felt deeply for Mary-Ann in her humiliation. She was right: Virgil Gipson was a pig, and then some — chiefly, a dangerously devious man whom he figured was working to an agenda of his own rather than in the interests of his deceased millionaire boss's estate, or the unfortunate man's lovely but now helpless daughter.

Additional horses were fetched from Pelzer's livery stable, a pack-horse to carry equipment, and mounts for Tom, Jed, Mary-Ann and Ernst. Tom was given his own trusty black gelding; Carbone a docile chestnut mare. Mary-Ann's calico animal was a well-broken, seven-year-old range horse from Texas, Pelzer said.

'Right, George,' he went on. 'Time's

a-wasting. Lead the way.'

No trust was placed in Tom or Jedidiah Carbone's co-operation. Before the ride began, both had their wrists tied with tough cord by the two rogue lawmen, Searle and Ernst. Their legs were fastened under their horses' bellies.

They took the trail out of town at a regular lope. Nansen Ernst brought up the rear, reduced once more to a scowling secondary role in proceedings. It fell to him to see that the prisoners kept up with the other eager riders.

Tom had a hard time. Experienced rider though he was, he found it difficult to keep steady in the saddle, especially not being able to make use of the stirrups.

Out toward the Tolley farm, the country sloped upward, rising higher through brush and strewn boulders to stands of larger growth, dominated by pine.

Searle called out, 'Keep those laggards moving, Nancy!'

'Y-you hear the man. H-hurry up, will you?'

Carbone grumbled, 'What they're going to see won't be running away, Deputy.'

'Easy, friend,' Tom told Ernst. 'You mightn't know it yet, but I reckon we could end up on the same side in this situation.'

The summits of the distant mountains formed a hard-edged skyline as the eastern sky grew lighter with the approach of sun-up. Then the rising sun fired up the horizon and washed the landscape with bands of shadow and brilliant colour — purple and red and gold.

Mary-Ann sat very erect, her blue eyes glistening. Tom wondered if, in spite of all, she was thrilled with the sight of this young and rugged land from which he had sprung and which he loved.

Searle wheeled his horse. 'Come on, back there! We ain't thumping our asses to gape around.'

'Your horse is starting to fret, Sheriff,' Tom said. 'Isn't it about time you three in front gave your beasts a rest? You've been pushing them all night, off and on, and they scarcely had time for a breather in Soldier Creek.'

Virgil Gipson said, 'I second that, Mr Searle. Not because I've any time for a Reb's opinions, but what he says seems right.'

Yeah, Tom thought. And maybe it'll give you a moment or two to figure out which way this cookie is going to crumble . . . and how you're going to get your mitts on the biggest of those crumbs.

Searle caught Pelzer's eye, and Tom saw the uncomfortable mayor give him a brief nod. The party stopped their horses to let them blow.

Gipson said, 'Gold's one hell of a lure, Mr Pelzer. But mining it is a tricky business. It'll take capital and expertise, you know.'

'I do, Mr Gipson, I do,' Pelzer said stiffly.

'I don't doubt your personal wealth in Soldier Creek terms is substantial,' Gipson pressed on, 'but you could be looking at a large initial capital investment of, say, three million dollars prior to realizing a return.'

'If the Charters estate can't provide it, I'm sure someone else will. Financial backing by well-to-do absentee investors and banks is common in your line of business, isn't it, Mr Gipson?'

Gipson didn't answer. 'And you'll need labour, both skilled and unskilled. Pickmen and powder monkeys.'

Pelzer grunted. 'We'll find it, recruit it. Whatever it takes.'

'You'll have to look to immigrants, for sure. The best might be hard-rock deep miners from Cornwall — men with skills developed over the centuries in Cornish tin and copper mines. But there'll be others, too, most likely. Serbs, Croats, Italians, Welsh, Germans, Irish . . . There'll be fights in such an open melting pot, wars even.'

The pair's exchange put Tom in mind

of two cur dogs warily circling one another before leaping into a scrap.

'Are you warning me or something?' Pelzer asked, eyes narrowed in suspicion.

Gipson gave his square chin a jerk. 'Why, no, just advice is all, Mr Mayor. Make what you like of it, pray do. Sheriff Searle here will find his bailiwick a hugely different place if it should all happen. Could be none of you would survive. I know about these things, you see. I've been there before.'

He finished with a grin. Faces were all growing haggard with the passing hours and growing stress. The grin was death-skull humourless.

Tom decided to chuck in his own two-pennyworth. 'Don't I get a say in any of this? We're talking about the *Tolley* farm here, remember?'

'Far as I recall, your pa never filed any mineral claims,' Pelzer said. 'Besides, the deeds of the place are now in my hands.'

'I don't know what became of my

father's papers, Pelzer. I was only four when Pa settled on the land. All the family records would have gone up in smoke, I figure, when the house was burned down by some of your good citizens.'

Tom was working up a good head of steam for his protests. Like everyone, he'd lost a night's sleep and the manner in which he was forced to ride was deucedly uncomfortable. 'Some other judge before your Yankee feller would have allowed my pa's prior claim to the land, if only because it was established by right of possession. Howsoever, I don't rightly understand legal shenanigans, or how the title passed to you.'

Carbone said quietly, 'But I've got a handle on them, Tom. You know and I know, Mr Pelzer, that you're skating on thin ice here.'

'That'll do, thank you, Mr Carbone, if that is your real name,' Pelzer snarled. 'You've got your own problems to look to. First, you have to prove you are the mining expert you claim. Next, you've got to clear yourself of suspicion of Mr Charters's murder.'

'Oh, I see,' Carbone said. 'When you've got what you want out of me, you'll put a rope around my neck and jerk on it, is that it? Or maybe it'll be a bullet in the back while escaping lawful arrest?'

'It c-could happen,' Ernst said, trying to make his presence felt. He pointed his pistol meaningfully.

'Well, Nancy,' Searle jeered. 'Ain't you the tough little law puppy?'

'This is disgusting, horrible!' Mary-Ann said. 'I can't believe what's going on here.'

'Don't listen to it,' Tom told her. 'I reckon most of it's bullshit anyway — beg pardon for the language.'

Searle lifted his sloping shoulders. 'Get back on those horses,' he told those who'd been able to dismount. 'There's been chinwag enough for a ladies' sewing circle, damnit.'

'Careful, George,' Pelzer said. 'No call to get testy.'

With a scrape and a clatter, the horses' hoofs came to a stop on the patch of weed-littered crushed rock that was the yard of the abandoned ruin of the Tolley farmhouse.

'Now, Mr Carbone,' Pelzer said. 'Time for you to begin showing your bona fides.'

'Sh-shall I untie him so he can t-take 'em off?' Ernst asked.

'Eh?' Tom said.

'God above!' Searle roared. 'The mayor ain't talking about clothes, stupid. He means for Carbone to lead us to where he reckons the ore is. Just unlash his feet. Tolley's, too.'

Ernst's cheeks turned crimson, but his eyes flashed with annoyance. 'Wh-why didn't he s-say so?'

Viciously, he slashed at the cords with a knife, careless of the cuts he inflicted on the skin that covered the bones of their ankles.

Tom swung a leg over the front of his

saddle and slipped to the ground. He groaned as he hit the ground. He ached to the bone in every muscle. Tired before they'd started out, he now had to cope with the effects of the unnatural, rigid posture he'd had to adopt to keep himself balanced upright in the saddle without the use of hands and feet. The predawn chill in the air had not helped any either. His features screwed up in pain as he straightened his back.

He glanced across at Carbone and Mary-Ann.

The Pinkerton man, out of disguise, was one of those rare people who possessed the kind of face it was possible to keep as blank as unused writing paper. Tom wouldn't even call it a poker face. But he knew Carbone must be aching just as he was.

Mary-Ann had fared better, not being tied. But her milky complexion was a degree or two paler. When her eyes met his, he saw they were full with what he took to be concern at his plight. Or was he fooling himself? No, he didn't think so. And notwithstanding his myriad pains, his heart took an involuntary jump of joy.

But that was a crazy trail to go down, he told himself, taking hold of his inappropriate feelings. Not just because of their present perilous situation, but because she was an heiress and he was just a landless farmer — worse, an unforgiven greyback for whom there was no pardon in this untamed country that he called his home.

'You're hurting, Tom, I can tell,' she whispered, as his unsteady steps took him past her. 'We've got to get away from this pack of maniacs. We must!'

'It wouldn't work,' he muttered. 'We both know it. It wouldn't work.'

Mary-Ann's look at him was searching, as though she knew he wasn't responding to her whispered injunction but answering an unspoken question — and that it was important to her she should know what it might be.

13

The Treasure Cave

The horses were picketed close by the wood where Carbone had once hidden his burro and began munching at a small patch of sparse grass.

Virgil Gipson supervised the unloading of the pack horse. He made a fuss over the several bull's-eye lanterns that had been brought along, fiddling with the metal-slides, and a bigger fuss over the experimental materials sent from the Charters mining operation in North San Juan.

'Steady with those explosives, Sheriff,' he warned.

Pelzer said brusquely, 'George knows about the unpredictability of such things. In Soldier Creek, we have an ordinance against the storing of nitroglycerine and gunpowder within town limits.'

'Right, Carbone,' Gipson said, when he was about as half as satisfied as the mayor was with himself, 'where do we get into this cave system?'

Carbone shrugged. To Tom, he said, 'Doesn't seem like I've got a choice, friend.'

Searle said, 'Mr Pelzer's told you the right of it, mister. Lead on.'

Carbone nodded in the direction of the slope and the tumbled rocks where the hell-raiser Al Jones and his pards had made their last stand.

'Up there, where some fool's lately fired the brush, God knows why. The tunnel that leads to the cave in question begins behind that ridge of red rock that looks like a rampart.'

Tom stumbled as he surveyed the changes to the vegetation, which were a mystery to him other than that they'd been wrought by a new fire. He cursed.

'Hadn't you better untie our wrists, too? Carbone and me are liable to fall flat on our faces. There's loose scree and Lord knows what else under that burned stuff. Moreover, as I remember it's no easy going inside the caves.'

Searle sniffed, wrinkling his nose and upper lip and twisting the absurd smudge of moustache that adorned it.

'Yeah . . . ' he decided. 'Do it, Nancy. There's no way they can get away. We'd shoot the Reb down like the dog he is before he could reach a hoss.'

Ernst produced his knife again. Tom thought about taking a swing at his jaw the moment his numbed hands were loose and making a determined dash for freedom. But he saw that the sheriff was right. He'd be cut down sure as shooting in the ructions that would set off.

Mary-Ann said, 'I take it you know the caves of old, Tom.'

'Not as well as Mr Carbone, it seems,' he said ruefully.

'I don't understand that.'

'They're a right labyrinth and full of danger — like rotten rock apt to fall on you and underground pools deep enough to drown in. As a boy, I used to go in with the stubs of old candles. But Pa said I'd get lost in all the twists and turns. He threatened to tan my hide if he had to come and haul me out. He told spooky windies, too — full of devils and witches and suchlike. One was about the vindictive spirit of a dead Indian shaman he called Head Crusher.'

Mary-Ann summoned the ghost of a smile. 'There's a few heads here could do with crushing.'

'You've got a smart mouth, Mary-Ann,' Gipson said. 'Shut it up is my advice. Hitch your wagon to the right horse and maybe you'll get out of this alive.'

'Up by those piles of old rags,' Carbone directed the climbing party.

And then, seeing the pulpy, reddened heaps, Mary-Ann screamed. 'They're *men*! They *were* men.'

Searle laughed derisively. 'Not a pretty picture, are they? The coyotes have had a chew on them already, I guess. They're the scum we shot and didn't have time to bury when we came out here afore, looking for your dirty friend Mr Carbone.'

'See?' Gipson said. 'That's what could become of you.'

The grisly remains of Al, Zeke and Wyatt had been dragged this way and that by the eager varmints who'd fed on them. Tracks of blood had been left across the rocky outcroppings. A head had been snapped off from one corpse at the neck and lay where it had rolled, lodged against a boulder, eyes still open, intact and staring in the sightless-ness of death.

'Look the other way, young lady,' Pelzer said. 'The buzzards will come today and clean up the rest of this mess.'

'Oh, God,' Mary-Ann said. 'I think I'm going to throw up.'

Tom felt sick himself. As light and warmth returned to the land, droning black swarms of flies were winging in and alighting on the smelliest parts of the chaos.

191

They scrambled up and over the boulders to a break in the stone face that soared up behind them. The gloom inside the cave entrance turned to profound darkness less than a dozen yards in. Tom was aware they were entering a black hole in the ground that angled down, possibly for miles.

The lamps were lighted before the bizarre party of treasure seekers went on, heads ducked, Carbone prodded forward to take the lead.

A solitary roosting bat, disturbed by the light, swooped low past their heads. Tom heard the beat and flurry of the stretched skin attached like wings of dark leather to its elongated fingers. He glimpsed a silver-frosted, furry tail.

Mary-Ann shivered. 'This is crazy. We must be stark, staring mad,' she muttered. But only Tom was listening anymore to what she had to say.

Rounding a sharp corner, Carbone paused, stooped some more and picked up a scrap of white cotton cloth. 'Hello,' he said. 'This looks new.

Someone's been in here since me. What do we make of it?'

'Nothing,' snapped Pelzer. 'A piece of shirt maybe, or a lady's petticoat. This crouching over is killing my back.'

'Another bit of rag ain't nothing significant,' Searle said impatiently. 'It might've blown in here. Drop it and push on, Carbone. We want to see this find of your'n.'

'Strange . . . ' Carbone shook his head, puzzled, but resumed his plodding progress into what seemed like the bowels of the earth.

The atmosphere was growing dank and foul now, much as Tom remembered it from his boyhood. A sense of claustrophobia he'd forgotten also crept over him. He wondered if it affected the others, or if they were too eaten up with their dream of a fabulous wealth lying ahead to notice.

Tom quickly lost track of time and sense of direction. The tunnel did not run straight for long. It twisted and turned abruptly, wrapping left or right around odd angles of different-coloured rock. Sometimes the way was wet underfoot and moisture brushed from the low ceiling by his hair trickled coldly down his neck.

When the tunnel met with another or was intersected, Carbone was unfaltering in the choices he made, like an ant crawling through the complexities of its run.

A gut feeling told Tom he was in for the surprise of his life. He was going to witness something remarkable which had stayed hidden from himself and his father in all the years they'd walked over this land that had been part of the Tolleys' acres.

Even Carbone hurried forward now. Tom thought it was something more than wanting to have this over with that propelled the mining expert's urgent steps. He was less cautious and staggered once or twice, then found steadier footing as the tunnel roof above them lifted higher, giving them room to raise their heads.

The bobbing lanterns cast waving beams of light across the tunnel. Though the tunnel had started to widen, the walls looked as close as ever. Grotesque shadows danced across them, like subterranean monsters threatening to pounce on them and extinguish the illumination that was their origin in a kind of eerie murder-suicide.

Tom would have understood if Mary-Ann — or indeed any of them who'd had no taste of caving before — lost their courage and fell to screaming as their only release.

All at once, they arrived. They found themselves in a natural vault, maybe twenty feet high and as much across in every direction. Everyone stood in a clammy silence broken only by the echoing drip of water from a distance. The beams from the lanterns, concentrated by the slides, moved across the fissured walls and jagged ceiling.

And they saw cold fires sparkle.

The fires were the lantern light

caught and reflected back by huge chunks of embedded quartz. Gold and silver ores veined and patterned the rock surrounding them. Underfoot, a huge reef of gold ore thrust up through the floor, a canted wedge of mineral wealth.

Tom was awestruck.

'Son of a bitch!' Gipson said. 'I ain't ever seen the like of it — a cave of gold. We're gonna be the richest guys in the world!'

Nansen Ernst picked a chunk of rock off the floor between his feet. He tossed it excitedly from hand to hand. 'I s-swear it's a nugget of gold! We'll be set up for l-life.'

It was the first time Tom had seen the young deputy purely elated.

Searle did a small jig on a slide of crumbled rock, like a fist-fighter who'd won a great victory.

'We must put in charges and blast out some prime samples,' Gipson said. 'I can't wait to see the assayers' reports on this stuff. We have to drill three holes about eighteen inches deep in the rock face — '

'Calm down, you dumbheads,' Carbone said. 'I've a feeling some people here haven't heard that a little knowledge is a dangerous thing. Much of the rock roundabouts is rotting and unstable. I think — '

'Doesn't matter what you think, Mr Expert,' Gipson said. 'I've got this new-fangled Swedish invention, remember? Not plain old blasting powder. Anyhow, we don't need you anymore. You and Tolley can die — simply disappear — the victims of some unknown accident or disagreement between you.'

Mary-Ann was indignant. 'If you think I'm going to witness murder and ignore it, Virgil Gipson, you're mistaken!'

'Huh! Then you can die with 'em, dearie. I don't need the Charters millions any longer. And I can buy a thousand women a lot fancier and higher-toned than you with the quarter share of what I see here.'

Pelzer drew himself up. 'Now hold on. We need to straighten out this matter of shares before we go any further. This mine is going to be on my land. I reckon I should get the biggest share and the most say.'

'You what!' Gipson screeched back. 'Don't you realize, Mr Puffed-up Mayor, that if it weren't for me your title to the land would be in serious question?'

'I do not,' Pelzer responded stiffly.

'Well, it's a fact. Huey Charters got a sniff of this find and favoured dealing with young Tolley here despite his Reb leanings. He had qualms about your rights, it seems. It was me who was all for backing you. I told Charters bluntly — a deal with you would be easier all round because you had the political power in this country. I was your finest advocate.'

Pelzer remained unconvinced. 'You're poor shakes as a liar, Gipson.'

'I'm not positive I appreciate your name-calling, Mr Mayor, 'specially after all I've done for you.'

His hard face took on a glowing, satanic shine in the weird artificial light.

'Charters wouldn't listen to me, so for your sake and mine I got him drunk and popped the cap that killed him in his open, snoring mouth. Thataway, I take control of his pesky daughter and all his business interests. The last two things don't matter now I've seen what's — '

He was interrupted by a wail of anger and grief. Mary-Ann threw herself at him — a spitting, hitting, scratching, kicking tornado of female fury.

'I should've known it all along, you bastard! It was you who murdered my pa! I hate you!'

14

Blown to Hell!

Searle and Ernst rushed to grab the distraught girl and haul her off Gipson, denying her the vengeance she couldn't hope to inflict with her puny physical powers. Tom was learning Mary-Ann Charters had great reserves of courage, yet no one could say she was a muscular woman.

But the disturbance, full of sudden movement and high emotion in the dimness outside the focused beams of the lanterns, gave Tom a chance he seized. In the jostle of bodies, he dipped his hand to Searle's tied-down holster. His hand closed around walnut grips and he deftly lifted out the .44, Model 1858 Remington revolver.

The lawmen dumped Mary-Ann into a corner, where she crumpled like an old coat. She was past tears, but great sobs welled up in her throat, her shoulders heaved, and she carried right on yelling.

'God, I hate you, Gipson! You're a foul and wicked man. Arrest him, Sheriff! He must go before a court and be hanged.'

Tom crouched to comfort her, concealing the stolen gun on the floor of the cave behind her. 'I'll see the skunk swings, Mary-Ann, if it's the last thing I do.' Boldly, he gave her shoulder a gentle, reassuring squeeze.

'I'll be all right in a minute,' Mary-Ann said, shaking with frustrated rage.

Searle scowled. He had a decision to make.

'Act smart, Sheriff,' Gipson said. 'We're all playing for bigger stakes here than a man ordinarily sees in a lifetime.'

'G-go for the g-gold,' Ernst urged.

Greed won out over conscience and the call of justice.

'I don't need your advice, you damned

young whipper-snapper,' Searle told his deputy with a snarl. Then he addressed the others. 'Nor will I let that little dramatic scene bother me overmuch, gents. We've come here to do another job of work, ain't we?'

Gipson, who was straightening his rumpled clothes, quickly pushed back his mussed-up hair, and dabbed at the bloody scratches on his face. 'That's very good, Sheriff, very good.' He produced a drill from his pack.

'Like I was saying, three holes . . . Then we pack a small stick of explosive into each, pushing it in deep as possible with a rod. On top of that, goes a length of fuse.'

With Gipson claiming the attention of his co-conspirators, Tom acted. Producing the Remington, he came to his feet and horned in.

'You can hold it right there, the four of you,' he said. 'If Searle is ducking his responsibilities, that leaves just Carbone and me to do the job. To arrest Virgil Gipson for murder and take the rest of you in as — '

He thought he had the situation under control till out of the tail of his eye he caught a movement by Pelzer. The mayor, who was standing slightly apart from the others, maybe nursing his grievance over the size of his share in the fortune before them, had a hand under his coat tail. Suddenly, he produced it, containing a small pistol.

Only swift reflexes saved Tom. The ball from the sneak gun plucked at his sleeve before hitting the rock behind him, ploughing a groove before it fell to the cave floor, its force spent.

Pelzer wasn't so lucky. The instant heavier roar of the Remington smothered the echoing crack of the smaller gun, and the bullet smashed into his chest.

Tom was a mite surprised at the effectiveness of his shooting. He'd heard that the conformation of the Remington's grip could cause problems for shooters with larger hands and used to the Colt. The angle and depth of the grip was definitely different and the trigger was wider and centred in the frame. He'd had to aim for the larger body mass, knowing a tricky disarming shot with the unfamiliar gun was beyond his ability and might only prove fatal to himself if unsuccessful.

Hit, Mayor Pelzer gave a convulsive jerk. His back arched, and he rose up on the balls of his feet, turning. Then the hideout pistol dropped from his suddenly limp fingers, and he pitched headlong and lifeless to the floor.

Into the sudden hush came a harsh laugh. Gipson said, 'Well, I guess the mayor's loss of life is our gain, Peace Officers. He was a fool to call me a liar about Charters. He'd had the evidence before his own eyes that Charters favoured paddling Tolley's canoe over his own. Wasn't it Charters who pushed him into letting Tolley go after he broke out of your jail the first time? Now Tolley's shot him. Serves him right, I say.'

Gipson's pitiless verdict was received

with a hysterical giggle. It was Nansen Ernst, his reason finally pushed over the edge into a kind of insanity.

'Ha-ha! p-pretty damned s-salty, the Reb! Now it's equal sh-shares for three, ain't it?'

'Goddamnit, you idiot, Nancy!' Searle said, groping disbelievingly at his empty leather and not minding his words too closely. 'He's still got my gun on us. What's more, it'll be a cold day in hell afore I go equal shares with any snot-nosed kid deputy like you.'

Ernst's face darkened as the blood rushed to it. Even now, it seemed Searle was his arch-enemy. He'd given him, Pelzer and Gipson the key to fabulous wealth. But still the Soldier Creek law boss treated him with sneering contempt — humiliating and insulting him before everyone, including an attractive young member of the opposite sex.

No wonder he'd snapped, Tom thought. But he didn't realize that the final reckoning was to be right now

205

until he saw the deputy draw his gun and point it straight and steady at the weaponless sheriff.

'Don't do it!' Tom cried. He was too late. The hammer dropped and his words were drowned out by the deafening crash of the .45.

The sheriff went down in a tumbling, sideways sprawl. A black hole, like a third eye, had appeared in his forehead, and he was a second man dead within the space of a minute. His two real eyes were fixed in a last wild glare, his mouth sagged open.

To the musty, underground atmosphere of the cave was added the reek of cordite.

Ernst shook his head sorrowfully. 'He p-pushed me inta it. Well, he ain't gonna c-call me Nancy no more — not n-never ag'in.'

'Oh, you damned fool,' Tom groaned. 'Will you put up that gun or are we two going to have to shoot it out?'

'Stop it — please stop the shooting!' Mary-Ann pleaded. 'You can't just kill one another like this. It will resolve nothing.'

She turned to Jed Carbone. Despite his background in crime and law enforcement with the Pinkerton Agency, he looked as stunned as anyone.

'Mr Carbone, tell them to desist. We've got to get out of this horrible place or I just know we'll all die.'

Virgil Gipson repeated her plea in a sarcastic tone. 'Oh, please stop the shooting . . . ' he mimicked. 'Touching, but what the hell does it matter, my dear? The more of these double-crossing hicks who die, the better it is for us.'

While Ernst was eyeballing Tom, Gipson was doing more than being satirical. He was also edging ever closer to the unhinged deputy. Finally, he made a lunge, closing the last few paces and smashing a fist full into Ernst's mouth, which sent the boy's head back to hit the rock wall, arms flung wide and high.

What his object was, Tom couldn't tell. Maybe he realized the odds had changed dramatically. He and Ernst were the only members left of the alliance to exploit the gold find. Could be he considered the young lawman might become more of an encumbrance than a help — a loose cannon best removed from the battle.

Ernst's gun went off again, discharging its second load into the cave's high ceiling. Shards of rock showered the occupants below.

Gipson caught hold of his flailing gun arm and tried to pull the weapon from his grip. But with vulnerabilities that made him a perfect victim for teasing, Ernst was long trained in the school of hard knocks. He knew how to defend and handle himself in a scrap if nothing else.

He hit Gipson on the right temple with a ham-like free fist. It was a smashing blow that jolted the older man and widened his hard eyes in surprise. Before Ernst could do it again, Gipson brought up his knee into his groin.

Ernst was twisting, however, and took some of the impact on his thigh. Yet he involuntarily lost his grip on the Colt. 'Aargh!' he grunted, and the gun flew end over end to the ground, exploding for the third time.

But with both hands free now, Ernst wasn't out of the fight. He was a big, strong boy. He bunched his right, gun hand into a second fist and, forcing his arm down despite Gipson's hold, which collapsed, slammed it hard on to the top of his head.

Gipson bellowed in sheer fury at the blow, which momentarily blinded him. He backed off, gathering his senses.

But Ernst gave him no quarter. He catapulted out from the wall, where he was somewhat cornered, in a deter-mined, windmilling rush that bore both men to the ground. They rolled this way and that, legs and arms thrashing wildly.

'Back,' Carbone rapped. 'This way, Tolley, Mary-Ann. There's another cave beyond this, through a smaller tunnel.

Bring a lantern and get out of these crazy sons' way.'

Tom considered ending the fight with another lethal bullet from Searle's Remington, but there was no telling what that might lead to. Gipson still had a gun at his belt, and either of them might end up in a position to pick up Ernst's revolver and reply in kind.

He didn't want to be the author of another death or dreadful injury . . . especially not of an appealing young woman who, one-time brat or not, heiress or not, had already suffered hugely in the past tumultuous day.

So he joined Mary-Ann and Carbone. They crawled on hands and knees into a still more confining tunnel than the one they'd come through to reach the treasure cave.

Tom turned, with difficulty, to watch the progress of the fight. It was going to be to the death, he thought.

The pair rolled over and over, exchanging vicious blows with balled fists. Neither one was going to let the other get to his feet and use the advantage of his boots. Once that happened, one man was going to have the living daylights kicked and stomped out of him for a certainty.

'I'll kill you!' Gipson screamed, driving a fist into Ernst's face so savagely that the boy had to spit out pieces of tooth from his bloodied mouth.

At that moment, Ernst's open hand, flung unseeingly to one side of him, happened to fall over the butt of his dropped Colt. Tom saw the desperation replaced with the light of hope in his eyes as he scooped the gun up and shoved the muzzle at Gipson's face.

Ernst's finger whitened as it curled tighter on the trigger. But at the last moment, Gipson again locked massive hands on his gun wrist and deflected the point of the Colt down, away from his face.

A fourth shot crashed out from the gun, a tongue of flame spitting from the muzzle in the gloom.

Tom never knew where the wild slug found its random target. It might have been one of the three fancy gunpowder sticks Gipson had been rigging up to procure his samples. It might have been something else in the pack he'd taken them from, abandoned on the cave floor.

Nor did Tom give the question consideration then, and afterwards it was forever unanswerable.

Every thought, every sensory perception and every feeling was completely extinguished by a deep, booming report. The cave was rocked by the enormity of the confined explosion.

The shock of the blast ran through the rock all around. Tom felt it pass through the very bones of his body.

From just behind him, where he crouched in the mouth of the smaller tunnel, came a shriek — Mary-Ann's terror adding to the shattering violence of the moment.

Then a tide of displaced air rushed into their tunnel, snuffing out the light in the single lantern brought there by Jed Carbone. In its wake rolled great clouds of choking smoke and fumes. Outside, in the cave, huge chunks of the roof started to fall.

My God, they've blown us all to hell, Tom thought. What a way to die.

The rumble of the subterranean thunder grew until it seemed his eardrums would split.

He flattened himself to the ground, face down and covering his head with his hands. But he still could hear the blast-tortured rocks tumbling and sliding and grinding against each other.

Tom lay in the darkness, expecting the life to be crushed out of him any moment. His breath rasped in his dust-lined throat. A man could experience no worse fear than this in a life of battle and strife.

The jarring and retching of the earth seemed set to go on forever. Tom thought the entire cave system would surely collapse from the shock waves. Then to his relief, if not his disbelief, the awful bedlam ceased.

He became aware of a heavy silence that pressed against his stressed eardrums. He spat out the dust in his mouth, and savoured the taste of his miraculous survival.

When Mary-Ann began screaming, he knew it was not sweet.

15

The Way Out

Mary-Ann was screaming like men he'd fought with during the war had screamed. Men who knew they were dying. Men gut-shot. Men who'd had limbs blown off and were watching their life's blood pump from the remnant stumps. Men who'd lost their minds.

'Mary-Ann!' Carbone shouted. 'Mary-Ann! It's all right — this tunnel's safe, we're alive. We'll get you out of here.'

Tom heard the change in pitch of her frantic cries and the chattering of her teeth as, he imagined, Carbone took a grip of her shoulders and shook her.

He groped around in the dense, gritty blackness with unsteady hands and found the lantern. Praise be! It was still upright and he heard the slosh inside it of unspilled fuel. He fumbled for matches and relit it.

The feeble flame fought to make an impression in the slow-swirling clouds of reddish grey dust. Carbone now had his arms round the girl, whose wails reduced to gasps for breath as light of sorts was restored.

Tom longed for his head to clear and his ears stop ringing from the blast and Mary-Ann's screaming.

She was taking control of herself at last, shamefaced, contrite. And Tom was powerfully glad of that.

'Sorry, sorry,' she said hoarsely between panting. 'I had to let it out. It was bad enough before the explosion and the blackness. But then it was a nightmare. I'm still hearing the roar of falling rock. What happened?'

Carbone coughed drily to shift the throat-clogging dust and wiped grit from his eyes. 'Those Swedish inventions your pa shipped in did their stuff in spades, is what happened.'

Gamely, Mary-Ann attempted a

retort. 'Pa said they were only dangerous when handled negligently.'

Tom said, 'Well, I guess shooting a
.45 slug into the darned box of tricks is
a heap negligent.'

'I could laugh, too, if our position
here wasn't so grave,' Carbone said. 'I
think we'll find our way back out of our
late company's treasure cave has been
well and truly blocked.'

'Can't we go on down this tunnel?'
Mary-Ann asked, freshly alarmed.

'No, we can't. I've got this whole
place mapped in my mind. There's just
a smaller cave — a dead-end, I'm
certain of that. I brought us in here
solely in search of cover from stray
gunfire, remember?'

Tom was hurt and bruised all over.
His face was cut and bleeding. Unlike
Carbone and Mary-Ann, who'd been
behind him, further into the tunnel,
he'd taken the brunt of the hail of
smaller rock fragments, spattered every
which way through the enclosed space
of the cave by the blast.

Realization they were alive had helped alleviate his minor pains. That comfort was now eliminated by a surge of fear. They were alive — but trapped.

★ ★ ★

The next step was to examine what was left of the cave and assess their options. If they could find any.

The dust in the air began to thin as it settled. 'Let's see how bad it is,' Tom suggested.

Underfoot, about half the floor of the cave appeared to be occupied by a crater. But this was difficult to determine, since much of the roof had collapsed and the hole was filled by fallen debris so that its full extent was obscured. A great mass of rock was heaped from floor to ceiling.

As had been feared, the entrance by which they'd reached the cave was also completely blocked by the piled-up rock.

Mary-Ann pointed to a human arm

extended from under the great stack of fallen rubble. 'Look!' she said, recognizing a big hand and the cloth of a coat sleeve. 'I think it's Virgil Gipson.'

Tom grimaced. The rest of the man's body must be hopelessly crushed under the rock slide. 'It couldn't have been a pleasant death.'

'He wasn't a pleasant man,' Mary-Ann said without sentiment.

Carbone said, 'If ever evil has engineered its own destruction, it has today.'

'Three others are buried under there, too,' Tom said. 'Not one of them could I much admire, but this makes 'em a gloomy, Godless tomb.'

Carbone coughed again, still finding difficulty with ingested dust. 'I hate to mention this, but even though we don't have the watches to tell us, time is ticking on and we're going to have to act without delay unless we want the place to be our tomb as well. This pocket appears completely sealed off. That means the amount of air is limited, and such are the circumstances that have led to any number of classic mining disasters.'

Mary-Ann's voice shook a little as she asked, 'What do you mean? What's going to become of us?'

'We're in a race against time, to put it bluntly,' Carbone said. 'Unless we can dig our way out of here, our breathing, our movements and the lantern will use up the oxygen in the enclosed, limited supply of air. Then we'll all die of suffocation. It'll be a toss-up, perhaps, whether the lantern will run out of oil first — but that's how we'll meet our end, in darkness or feeble light. Our lungs, starved of air, will begin to burn. The linings of our throats will swell and seem to close up until we claw at them in desperation.'

'What a horrible way to go!' Mary-Ann cried. 'We must try to dig ourselves out while we still have the light.'

'God, what I wouldn't give for a pick and shovel,' Tom said.

'I'm sorry, son. It's bare hands or nothing,' Carbone said.

Tom tried to force some cheer into his voice, if only to bolster Mary-Ann's sorely tried spirits. Her drawn face was still beautiful, but the vitality he'd first observed in it was depleted without her merry smile.

'Hands it is then. If it works, I might live to become a miner yet.'

He put a foot on to the rubble and tentatively reached for holds higher up. 'Maybe I can clear a narrow hole near the top and crawl over into whatever's left of the tunnel.'

'That's the idea,' Carbone said. 'Hand me the rocks you pull out and I'll toss them back.'

But Tom had to climb the rock slide first and it was far from easy. For every other foothold he gained, another proved treacherous. He added a twisted ankle and more cuts to his injuries. His fingers were soon bloody; the nails torn ragged, the knuckles skinned.

The atmosphere was thick and

growing hotter, so that his shirt stuck to his sweat-streaked back.

Yet the mental torments were worse than the physical. For each rock he removed and passed down to Carbone, thousands remained piled ahead. And there was the pressing knowledge that light and air were not limitless.

How soon before they were plunged absolutely into a black, suffocating void?

It was precarious work, even more difficult than Tom had supposed. He would pull out what looked like a big rock and the space would be filled instantly by a slide from above it. Shards of shattered stone were constantly trickling over his feet; bouncing off his head and shoulders from above.

He was beginning to feel that the task was hopeless, that they were doomed, when he felt a coolness caress his forehead. It reminded him of the hand of his mother when he'd been a boy and had suffered a fever. Was he starting to imagine things? Was this how it was when you went crazy?

'Do you feel anything?' he called down to the others, his voice shaking.

'Feel what, Tom?' Mary-Ann said.

'Nothing to be felt, son,' Carbone said, a bit gruffly. 'You're getting tired is all. Maybe we'd better change places. There can't be much time left us.'

'No, hand me up the matches, will you?'

He struck a sulphur tip against the rock and a tiny flame leaped into life. When it was burning steadily, he lifted it above his head and watched in fascination.

The flame wavered, then bent, as though pulled by an unseen current. Light-headed though he was becoming, he didn't believe it could be the blown breath of a subterranean troll from one of his pa's ghostly tales.

'There's fresh air getting in!' he exclaimed. 'We can survive down here after all.'

'Why, that's great news, Tom,' said Carbone, but quickly added a caution.

'Now we've only got to break through before the lantern gives out, and to beat thirst and hunger.'

The first match sputtered out, singeing his numbed fingertips, and Tom used another to find the source of the air percolating through the gaps in the obstructing rock pile.

He began to concentrate his rock-shifting efforts at the point of the air's entry and made better progress. But it was still alarmingly slow and tiring work. He didn't think he would be able to keep it up till he made a breakthrough. Trickles of unstable rock kept falling, too, thwarting his efforts — sometimes, it seemed, even nullifying them.

Carbone realized he was dog-tired and that what he was doing in that state might prove counterproductive.

'Call it off for a while. We know there's air coming through and we can last that bit longer. I think we should turn out the lantern and give ourselves some rest, if not a sleep. Then we might be able to tackle it with renewed energy.'

'Yes, Tom,' Mary-Ann said. 'I dread to think what another big cave-in would do. I could bear waiting a little longer now, especially if we could work on the task more safely and effectively later.'

Tom nodded dumbly. He didn't have the strength to speak, let alone argue. He slipped and stumbled down the slide of loose rock and gratefully sat down with the others. Carbone extinguished the lantern.

The thick darkness was frightening at first, but Tom soon gave in to his fatigue, let his eyelids droop — though there was nothing but total blackness to shut out — and dozed.

He had no idea how long he'd slept when an unrecognizable clink broke through the mists of troubled sleep to his consciousness. It was hardly louder than a clock tick in the dense silence. Was the rock on the move again? He was instantly alert. But it wasn't that.

This was too regular and too distant

to be the new cave-in Mary-Ann feared.

'Listen!' he rasped, shaking the others to wakefulness.

'By God!' Carbone said. 'I do believe I hear the sound of metal on stone. After all my years in mining I couldn't mistake that, anywhere. People with tools are coming to dig us out.'

The sound was growing more persistent and closer. Hope flooded through them.

Mary-Ann said, 'It's unbelievable. Tell me I'm not dreaming, will you? How can anyone in the outside world have known we're here?'

'Maybe they don't, really,' said Tom. 'I figure we should start shouting for all we're worth before they give up on the job.'

'Smart thinking, young man,' Carbone said. 'Let them know we're here and need rescuing.'

'But who can it be?' asked Mary-Ann, before she fell to yelling without waiting for an answer. 'This way! We're here! Here, down in the cave!'

Finally, after a full minute of concerted shouting, they heard a reply.

'Tom Tolley! Ees that you in there, Tom?'

* * *

Tom blinked as he emerged into the sunlight and was momentarily blinded by the brightness. He'd never found an Arizona sky so blue, or so welcome.

The small crowd gathered on the slope that went down to the burned-out Tolley homestead was mainly Mexican. So was the small army of rescuers with picks and shovels led by Carlotta Menéndez and her brother Pedro.

The people waiting below raised a ragged but joyful cheer as Tom, Mary-Ann and Jed Carbone came into sight on the rocky promontory outside the cave mouth above them.

Tom felt warm and glad inside and waved to acknowledge their salutation. 'But, Carlotta,' he demanded at last, when he could hold back his bewilderment no longer, 'how did you know we were there?'

Fussing over his scrapes and bruises, Carlotta told him the story of her capture by the three hardcases, Al, Zeke and Wyatt.

'It was very terrible, Tom. They brought me here and Mayor Pelzer and Shereeff Searle came. There was much gonfire and the brush, it was set alight, making a beeg smoke. The beeg ugly man who came to town with Señor Charters jumped up like a jack-in-the-box devil and he fire at me. But I am very lucky. His bullet only glance off my head. What you say? It crease my skull. I crawl into cave and hide. I am very dazed, you see. I think I sleep.

'Then the shereeff and the mayor and the ugly man return with prisoners — you and the old hobo Carbone, and the young Charters lady.'

'Why didn't you show yourself?' Mary-Ann asked.

'I do not trust Shereeff Searle. He as

much in the mayor's pocket as that crook's gold watch. Soldier Creek is in their greep — they run the town, *sí*? They have been unkind to Tom, who is good to me and who I like. The ugly man, he has shot at me.

'So when I see they come to the cave, I run down to the woods by their *caballos* and hide and wait. Afterward, I hear big bang and see much dust puff from caves. I take *caballo* and go to town to fetch help.'

'Well, thank God you did,' Carbone said. 'Everything's explained, including the piece of torn cloth I found in the tunnel. Now I can stop being a hobo, get out of these filthy old clothes and look forward to civilized life in Chicago.'

Carlotta ruminated. 'You are very lucky to do that, *señor*. It was touch and go. For many hours we slave to clear the cave-in. We work most of the day digging you out.'

Tom looked around. 'Say, what time is it?'

'The sun is almost down,' Carlotta said, pointing.

'No wonder I'm hungry. I haven't had breakfast yet.'

'Ah, yes, breakfast. Would you like two fried eggs on tortillas? Topped with some stripes of salsa and melted cheese and tomato slices. And some strong, hot coffee, of course.'

'I surely would,' Tom said, his tastebuds coming to mouth-watering life.

'Mmm . . . sounds delicious,' Mary-Ann said. 'Make that order for two, please.'

But before they were to eat, the ex-Rebel and the heiress had much to talk about on their way back to town.

THE END

We do hope that you have enjoyed reading this large print book.

Did you know that all of our titles are available for purchase?

We publish a wide range of high quality large print books including:
Romances, Mysteries, Classics
General Fiction
Non Fiction and Westerns

Special interest titles available in large print are:
The Little Oxford Dictionary
Music Book, Song Book
Hymn Book, Service Book

Also available from us courtesy of Oxford University Press:
Young Readers' Dictionary
(large print edition)
Young Readers' Thesaurus
(large print edition)

For further information or a free brochure, please contact us at:
Ulverscroft Large Print Books Ltd.,
The Green, Bradgate Road, Anstey,
Leicester, LE7 7FU, England.
Tel: (00 44) **0116 236 4325**
Fax: (00 44) **0116 234 0205**

Other titles in the
Linford Western Library:

THE GUNS AT THREE FORKS

Terrell L. Bowers

The war between the Union and the Confederacy has ended, but the fight is not over for the Kenyon family. Being Yankees, their presence in Three Forks, Texas, is met with hostility and resentment. Dave Kenyon defies the odds and tries to court a local girl. Then he is forced to kill the cousin of a deadly bandit leader, Angel Gervaso, who vows revenge and sends his gang to burn Three Forks to the ground. The Union boys and pro-Confederate populace must now rally together against their common enemy . . .

BENDER'S BOOT

Mark Bannerman

Bloody Kansas, 1872, and Conroy McClure is searching for his missing brother. At a remote inn, he becomes involved with an evil family and, in particular, the she-devil of a daughter who ensnares men in a murderous web of sensuality. Local vigilantes storm the inn, intent on lynching the entire family. But the killers have fled, taking McClure with them. Buried in the adjacent orchard are twelve brutally mutilated bodies, including a little girl who was clearly buried alive. But what is the fate of Conroy McClure?

RED ROCK RENEGADES

David Bingley

When the South-Western Detective Agency took on the Strang case, Slim Blake believed that the outlaw Willie Marvin was alive. On a search for Willie he took a beating before leaving for New Mexico to contact the new client. Jason Strang often had tricksters after his money, but Edith Lamont was a 'grafter'. Working on the plot against Jason, Slim's life was endangered. Willie Marvin and his kidnappers had to be fought with bullets and guile in Red Rock Canyon before Jason could resume his ordinary way of life.